The Witch *of* Beaver Creek Mine

The Witch *of* Beaver Creek Mine

Rosemarie Nervelle

Down East BOOKS

ISBN (10-digit): 0-89272-741-1
ISBN (13-digit): 978-0-89272-741-4
Jacket illustration by Jim Sollers
Printed at Thomson-Shore Inc.

5   4   3   2   1

LIBRARY OF CONGRESS CATALOGING-IN-PUBLICATION DATA

Nervelle, Rosemarie.
    The witch of Beaver Creek mine / Rosemarie Nervelle.
        p. cm.
    Summary: In Beaver Creek, Nova Scotia, in 1942, thirteen-year-old Johnny
Lightfoot is helped by the disfigured woman called Old Maud, who is believed to
be a witch, and he sets out to become her friend and to let the other villagers
know that she is not to be feared.
    ISBN-13: 978-0-89272-741-4 (trade pbk. : alk. paper)
    ISBN-10: 0-89272-741-1
    [1. Hermits--Fiction. 2. Disfigured persons--Fiction. 3. Family life--Nova
Scotia--Fiction. 4. Healers--Fiction. 5. Micmac Indians--Fiction. 6. Indians of
North America--Nova Scotia--Fiction. 7. Superstition--Fiction. 8. Nova Scotia--
History--20th century--Fiction. 9. Canada--History--1914-1945--Fiction.] I. Title.
    PZ7.N437764Wit 2007
    [Fic]--dc22
                                            2007006452

Down East Books
A division of Down East Enterprise, Inc.
Publisher of *Down East*, the Magazine of Maine

Book orders: 1-800-685-7962 www.downeast.com
Distributed to the trade by National Book Network

In memory of my grandfather, John Cromwell,
whose own wonderful stories
were the wellspring for mine

To John's great-grandchildren, Michael and Kimberley;
and to his great-great-grandchildren,
Ashlee, Amber, Anthony, and Shannon

Author's Note

This story and its characters are fictitious and are not intended to portray any actual person or place. Some of the characters, however, are composites of people I knew as a child, born and raised in Nova Scotia, and include Micmac Indians, a tribal branch of the Algonquin Nation. As was common practice even before the 1800s, Micmacs intermarried with French, Scottish, and Irish immigrants and former slaves. They settled in Nova Scotia, New Brunswick, Newfoundland, Quebec Province, and Maine.

My grandfather, the product of just such intermarriage, was proud of his Micmac heritage. His mother was half French and half "black Micmac," a common name for children of Micmac and black parents; his father was also a mix of black and Micmac. All were born in Nova Scotia. His wife—my grandmother—was also born to an interracial couple. Her mother was an Irish lady who married a very handsome half-black and Irish gentleman. This dash of black on her father's side was most likely derived from the gene pool of African loyalists who gained their freedom by joining the British army and sailing with it from New York to Nova Scotia during the American Revolution of 1775.

The events in the story take place in 1942–43, when a great many Micmac Indian descendants had joined mainstream New England life by intermarrying with European descendants. They raised families and made their living mostly by farming and fishing. They were hard-working and respected members of their communities.

Some readers familiar with Mi'kmaq Indians might question my spelling of Micmac, but that's how it was spelled during the time of this tale. My grandfather once told me that the spoken word of greeting to some of the first Europeans in New England (the French) was "Nikmaq." It was pronounced *nick-mack*, with clicks at the back of the throat, and the word meant "brother." The French name for the Micmac Indians, M'kmaq, was derived from this Nikmaq greeting.

The early Micmacs had no written language, but used pictographs carved in stone or wood. Later, the original French word, M'kmaq, was spelled in several different ways: Mikmaq, Mikmak, or Mi'gmaq. The Micmac language was eventually written down using the same Roman alphabet that we use for English today. This was probably done by Jesuit missionaries to teach Christian prayers to Micmac converts. When my grandfather was born, in the late 1800s, "Micmac" was still the accepted spelling. It was easy to pronounce and spell, and everyone understood who was being talked about. Today, native speakers often refer to themselves as Lnu'k, the original Micmac word for "the people." After a 1980 television series entitled *Mi'kmaq*, museums all over New England began using the spelling Mi'kmaq, which is now considered the correct spelling.[1]

When all is said and done, if any reader were to ask me what I like best about Micmac Indian traditions, I would have to say their excellent storytelling capabilities. My grandfather was no exception. At different times a lumberjack, a trapper, and a hunting guide, he frequently told me about his life adventures, which provided the grist for his storytelling mill. Taking episodes from one story and blending them into another for heightened effect, he wove magical tales, the likes of which I'd never before heard, and you might never hear . . . unless I tell them to you.

Rosemarie Nervelle

---

1. Native Languages of the Americas: Mi'kmaq, *http://www.native-languages .org/Mikmaq.htm*

One

The train was still twelve minutes out from Beaver Creek station when the whistle blew several short, insistent blasts. The hot, weary passengers coming home from Saturday's marketing glanced curiously out the windows. Seeing nothing but the shadow of the moving train sliding through the scrub pine, aglow in the setting sun, they settled back into their seats and began to gather their belongings. Then suddenly, without further warning, came the grinding, piercing screech of the brakes.

Women screamed and grabbed their children. Passengers were thrown from their seats and men tried to catch packages falling from the overstuffed racks above. Bags of chicken feed burst open, spilling their contents over everything and everyone. Sacks of flour exploded in great white clouds, turning passengers into a jumble of ghosts with red-rimmed eyes. Freed from its smashed cage, a black and white chicken flapped and flew to the other end of the coach. When the train finally came to a stop, a grim-faced conductor rushed from the caboose, eyes popping at the devastation to his previously immaculate passenger coaches. He made his way through the crowded cars, checking for injuries.

Thirteen-year-old Johnny Lightfoot had slid forward off his seat and landed squarely in his Uncle Billy's lap in the seat opposite.

"Are you all right, Johnny?" Billy asked as they untangled themselves.

"I think so," Johnny replied, looking somewhat embarrassed.

Except for a few bruised shins and ruffled tempers, no one was seriously hurt.

"What happened?" Billy asked the conductor as he brushed flour from the shoulders of his jacket.

"It's Old Maud," the conductor replied. "She's on the tracks."

Everyone rushed to the windows, pushing and shoving to get a rare glimpse of the mysterious old woman. The train had stopped only a few yards from where she stood; her back was to the engine. Leaning from his open window, the engineer shouted something and waved his arms. Johnny saw Old Maud step off the tracks, then impatiently wave the train on its way as if swatting at a pesky mosquito, the sleeves of her raggedy garment flapping. Within seconds, she had disappeared into the woods, and the disgruntled passengers returned to collecting their scattered belongings.

It was 1942 in Beaver Creek, a small town thirty-five miles northwest of Halifax, Nova Scotia. The population of Beaver Creek had almost doubled, to 960, since the mid-1800s. Micmac Indians from eastern Canada, Irish and Scottish immigrants from Europe, descendants of African slaves, and French Canadians from Quebec had all come to work in the Beaver Creek gold mine. When the gold ran out and the mine closed in the late 1800s, most of the village's inhabitants were content to stay where they had made their homes and raised their families. Beaver Creek became a community of trappers, hunting guides, lumberjacks, shopkeepers, carpenters, and farmers who raised cattle and sheep—and fruit trees that could withstand the long, cold winters.

The citizens of Beaver Creek were a hard-working, family-oriented, rugged people. The women worked side-by-side on the farms with their menfolk until their children were old enough to take over their fair share of the chores. The women's hands were rough and gnarled; their bodies sinewy and agile. They drove teams of oxen, rode horses, chopped firewood, milked cows, raised chickens, and hauled well water.

In winter the girls played hockey with the boys after school on Bottomless Pond's pocked ice. In handed-down black hockey skates, they practiced fancy figure-eights like the famous Olympic figure skater Sonja Henie. Girls and boys alike fished, hunted for deer, partridge, and quail, and snared rabbits. They wore work clothes most days, and—except for the hottest days in summer—rubber boots with the tops turned down.

Beaver Creek families were large, and neighbors depended on one another to help keep track of the comings and goings of their children. There was only one doctor in the village, who mended broken bones, removed appendixes and tonsils, took stitches in cuts, and performed simple surgery. Two midwives delivered most of the babies. Only the complicated deliveries and the most seriously ill patients were transported to the hospital in Bedford.

The citizens of Beaver Creek came together at weddings, births, funerals, and monthly marketing days. Only on those days did the women wear dresses, along with sensible shoes and big, colorful kerchiefs that also served as covering for the head—a requirement when attending church on Sunday. Marketing day was an exciting opportunity for the women of Beaver Creek to experience what they considered sophisticated ladies in nearby Bedford, who wore high-heeled shoes and carried matching handbags.

In the milieu of life in Beaver Creek, each culture preserved its own legends, customs, and beliefs, but the one superstition they all shared was their fear of the mysterious old woman who lived in the mine.

Johnny Lightfoot had heard strange things about Old Maud from his friends at school. They eagerly repeated their parents' stories about the old lady's witchcraft and powerful medicine. By far the scariest tales, however, were the ones that Johnny had overheard in bits and pieces from local farmers around the potbellied stove at Milligan's Store. Where Old Maud had come from no one knew; nor did they know how long she had lived in the abandoned gold mine north of the village. Lately, though, she had been seen leaving the tracks at the railway crossing on Cobequid Road, carrying a kettle of berries, a snared rabbit, or a string of fish. Folks who lived along the road watched her suspiciously from behind their window curtains until she was safely out of sight.

Old Maud's appearance was as frightening as her reputation. Her back followed a curious curve, and her head protruded forward on her long neck. Thin white hair, usually matted with twigs and leaves, seemed to sprout in patches from her dark scalp. She was missing an eye, although it didn't seem much of a handicap. She wore a long black frock; in summer, the tattered hems of her skirts were dusty; in winter, they were crusted with snow and ice.

The entire community kept a safe distance from her. Although they called her Old Maud, no one had ever ventured close enough to guess her age. Nor did anyone really know how she came to be called Old Maud. She had lived in the valley as far back as anyone in Beaver Creek could remember. She was "ugly," they said, and they believed that with her one big eye she could see for miles, and even around corners.

Folks claimed that she had such strong powers that she could change into different animal forms to hunt at night. Once an old prospector, having stopped for supplies at Milligan's Store, told how he'd found heaps of bones at the mouth of a mine shaft, and how a large crow had flown so close over his head that he took a fright and ran all the way back to the village.

The old-timers said she could mix potions to kill or cure, although no one would swear to have witnessed her magic firsthand. Rumor had it that certain harsh parents threatened to summon Old Maud when their children misbehaved—a sure cure for talking back, even bed-wetting. Every unusual illness, unexpected death, and misfortune in the village that couldn't be rationally explained was blamed on Old Maud's evil doings.

Herb Norris, the government man and gatekeeper of the mine, lived in a little house at the bottom of Mine Hill. His job was to keep the inhabitants of Beaver Creek from trespassing on mine property. After the mine closed some fifty years before, sinkholes formed and some of the shafts collapsed. The government condemned the mine and sealed off the only legal entrance. Over the years, however, generations of villagers discovered different ways to enter the mine to hunt game or gold nuggets.

Lately, Old Maud's wanderings took her directly past Mr. Norris's gatehouse. As gatekeeper, he felt duty-bound to discover Old Maud's destination. She might even unknowingly lead him to a path she was using to secretly enter the mine. One day he watched her pass his gate and decided to follow her. He kept out of sight until she was quite a distance up Cobequid Road, just before Hubley's Bend, then he ran as fast as he could to the curve in the road. The long, open stretch of road before him was empty. She had completely disappeared! Herb felt his knees go weak. He spun quickly around to glance behind him, but he seemed to be alone on the road.

Herb's interpretation of job responsibility changed dramatically after that, especially concerning Old Maud. Although she often passed his house, he never again attempted to approach her. Why should I? he asked himself, then admitted the answer: She spooked him, as she did everyone else in Beaver Creek. But, he reasoned, as long as she minded her own business, he wouldn't interfere with her comings and goings. Let sleeping dogs lie. He felt comfortable with his decision.

Yet as the days grew shorter and cold weather arrived, Herb felt a growing compassion for the old woman who quietly passed his gatehouse without a sideways glance. A neighborly gesture on his part surely would demonstrate his friendly attitude toward her. He devised a plan. One night, in a shallow knothole of the big tree on her path, just past the gatehouse, he left a small packet: a can of soup, a tin of fish, a little tobacco. He marked its presence with a rabbit skin nailed to the tree so she couldn't miss it. He wondered whether she would be curious enough to investigate. He planned to watch from his darkened window, until he remembered that she could see in the dark. He decided not to spy on her, and went to bed.

Early the next morning he got up, dressed quickly, and went outside. The rabbit skin was gone. He reached into the knothole and, to his amazement, found a parcel wrapped in a scrap of cloth. He quickly carried it into the house and opened it. It held a small fragment of white stone containing a tiny gold nugget. Herb was moved. He had been right about Old Maud. He had offered her his friendship, and she had responded in kind. His heart smiled with happiness.

Herb told his story proudly, again and again, to an audience of spellbound villagers. But he was always careful not to reveal the whereabouts of the "secret" knothole.

Milligan's Store, sitting at the crossroads of Route 2 and Cobequid Road, was an important social meeting place. Villagers discussed everything about their lives, monumental and otherwise, public and private. One naked lightbulb hung from the tobacco-blackened tin ceiling. Sharing importance in Beaver Creek was community news, radio programs, weather, and world politics, including World War II, called Mr. Roosevelt's war after then-President of the United States, Franklin D. Roosevelt. The store, like every other general store in Nova Scotia in the 1930s and '40s, was a combination market: groceries, livestock feed, tobacco, hardware, a butcher shop, a post office, and a ticket agent for the Amherst bus to points north and south on Route 2. The bus stopped at the intersection only when Mr. Milligan put out the flag, and only when at least two passengers were going southeast to Halifax or north to Truro. At Truro, the bus turned west and then north again, making train connections from Amherst to Moncton and to Saint John, New Brunswick. Unlike the train from Windsor Junction, the bus carried no freight or livestock.

Every day the village children stopped at the store on their way home from school to buy penny candy, and to hear Mr. Milligan's recitation of everything in the store except what he knew they came for. "We've got whippin' cream, cold cream, sausages and ham, rice, barley, beans, ginger, pepper, cornmeal. What'll it be, kiddies?" They left with pockets filled with jawbreakers, BB-bats, honeymoons, and chewies—miniature sugar-coated slices of coconut patties colored to look like watermelon.

The door to the shop displayed chipped, but still colorful, advertisements for Coca-Cola, Old Dutch cleanser, and Oxydol. In the display window to the right of the entrance, among sun-faded boxes and tins whose withered white labels clung by a cor-

ner, were wool socks and work boots and the dusty rack of a
moth-eaten moose head. From the other window a disintegrating
stuffed bass of fairly good size gazed blindly at the passing traffic.
Once trophies, they were now merely mementos of Mr. Milligan's
past prowess as a hunter and rod fisherman. Old brown photographs lay curled and faded beside each relic. The potbellied stove
sat at the far end of the store, in front of the post office wicket,
behind which Mrs. Milligan, the postmistress, sat knitting. In
front of the stove were four old Windsor chairs positioned around
a large checkerboard on top of a cracker barrel, convenient for
anyone wishing to make the next move. It was here, around the
stove—winter and summer—that all the news changed hands and
the best yarns were spun. The stories were embellished and exag-
gerated, then retold at home by the light of a kerosene lamp.

Two

It was Johnny Lightfoot's thirteenth birthday the day that he and his Uncle Billy saw
Old Maud from the train window. They
were returning from the bank in Halifax,
bringing home their paid-up mortgage papers and the little ivory
mortgage "button" presented to them by the bank. The Lightfoot
family owned a sixty-eight-acre farm, one of the largest in the
valley. They raised more vegetables than they could use, so they
sold some and gave away the rest. They kept a few cows, some
chickens, two work horses, and a big, beautiful chestnut mare
named Ruby, which belonged to Billy Lightfoot. Fifteen acres of
the farm grew some of the best apples, picked and shipped to market every October.

For Johnny's birthday and for the "burning" of the mortgage
documents, Johnny's mother prepared a big celebration supper.
Johnny's favorite dish, largemouth bass, was stuffed and roasting
in the oven. The big fish had been caught by his grandfather that
very morning. The aroma assailed Johnny's nostrils as he opened
the kitchen door. A bright smile spread from ear to ear and his
heart warmed. He was happy to be home with his family gathered
ceremoniously around the big kitchen table: his parents, Nathan

and Mary; his grandfather Big John; his uncle Billy; a younger brother, Seth; and two baby sisters, Nell and Janie. The younger children could hardly contain their excitement about the chocolate cake hidden in the pantry, and about their carefully made presents for Johnny's birthday.

Big John proudly held up the traditional mortgage button and spoke. "To celebrate Johnny's birthday, I hereby bestow upon him, my firstborn grandchild, the honor of placing our mortgage button in the newel post." Big John explained this practice to the younger children. "All who enter our front door will know, when they see this ivory button in the newel post, that our mortgage has been paid in full."

Everyone applauded. All of Big John's children and grandchildren had been born on the Lightfoot homestead, and they were happy and proud that the farm was free and clear at last.

Johnny's father raised his hand for silence. He cleared his throat, stood tall, and appeared serious except for a twinkle in his eye. His voice was warm with pride and pleasure.

"We've been blessed by our Mother Earth with a fine farm in this rich valley of beautiful forests, sparkling water, and abundant game," said Nathan. "We have good land, a strong family, and much to be thankful for."

He turned to Johnny and held up a glass of apple cider. "Our family was proud the day you were born, Johnny. You are a wonderful son who stands on the threshold of manhood, and you grow taller and stronger every day. Ladies and gentlemen, this toast is for Johnny, who will begin tomorrow to share more of the responsibilities for the care and feeding of the Lightfoot family."

"Here, here," Billy piped up, smiling in agreement, while Seth, Nell, and Janie clapped their hands with glee.

Johnny laughed with the others. Although his father's jovial announcement meant that Johnny was expected to take on more of the farm chores beginning at five o'clock the very next morning, that didn't spoil his enjoyment of the evening.

The celebrations moved to the hearth, where Johnny described in great detail how, on his trip to Halifax with Billy, he had worked hard to extract every delicious morsel of lobster from its shell in the spectacular dining room of the Dorchester Hotel.

"Oh, but are you going to tell them how long it took?" asked Billy.

When the laughter died down, Johnny started to describe the train trip home. But he noticed a slight frown cross Billy's face, a signal to change the subject.

Later, when the little ones were in bed, Johnny's parents asked to hear what had happened on the way home that day.

The subject of Old Maud had never been discussed openly before. Nathan and Mary Lightfoot took care not to repeat village gossip of any kind in front of their children.

"There were only two coaches behind the engine today," Johnny began. "Uncle Billy and I were in the first one. The train suddenly braked and everything flew all over. The conductor told us that Old Maud caused the trouble. Most everybody rushed to the windows. She was on the tracks, Grandfather." Johnny moved nearer his grandfather to make sure he heard every word. "We could see her pretty close, but the light was fading and she had her back to us, so we couldn't see her face. Some of the folks wouldn't even look." Johnny laughed nervously.

Big John knew a few stories of his own about Old Maud and her spells and incantations. When Johnny finished, Big John slowly prepared his pipe, sucking the flame into the bowl, the shadows playing on his strong features. He lowered the wick in the kerosene lamp, and his voice grew deep and his eyes went dark.

"Old Maud is believed to have very special powers, indeed," he said slowly, quietly. "She has been known to cast spells on wicked folks—those who harm others. She has, in the heat of summer, mysteriously produced frost in flower gardens. She's caused roosters to abandon large flocks of prize hens, and bees to turn on their keepers. Lightning once struck thirteen fruit trees in a row on the same day. And I've heard that she once placed seven toads on a family's doorstep, casting a spell on the entire household, even the cat. On the other hand, when Mrs. McKay's baby was sick, Dr. LeBrun miraculously cured the child with medicine they say was concocted from Old Maud's herbs. Now, what do you think of that?"

"I'd say it took a bit of magic to keep all those toads in one place for any length of time," Billy offered mischievously.

Big John bit hard on the stem of his pipe to keep from laughing. Everyone enjoyed the clever joke except Johnny, who forced a halfhearted laugh. Deep down, he believed every word of what his grandfather said about Old Maud's evil side and doubted her "good" side. Thinking about it made the hair prickle on his neck.

Later that night when the party was over and Johnny climbed the dark stairs to his room with his dog, Chum, he made sure to turn the wick higher in the lamp he carried. Although Johnny enjoyed his birthday celebration, the stories about Old Maud were foremost in his mind.

Her name was not mentioned again for several weeks.

Johnny's thirteenth year was a year of "firsts" for him. He and his Uncle Billy target-practiced north of the Lightfoot apple orchards toward Loon Lake. Billy taught Johnny to track, to shoot, and to understand the habits of the animals they hunted for food. Nine years older than his nephew, Billy was tall, lean, and spirited. He wore his silky black hair long, tied back with a shoelace. He sometimes rode his mare without a saddle, and taught Johnny the fine points of caring for a horse. Johnny loved Billy and looked up to him like a big brother whose advice and experience he respected. He honored the strict rules that Billy expected him to abide by. Johnny was not permitted to take a gun into the woods to hunt alone, and he was forbidden to go into the mine.

Johnny's dog, Chum, was a broad-chested, mixed bulldog mutt with "liver" spots on his short white fur. He was an odd-looking dog—his tail was never bobbed—but he was smart. He was a good pointer with a fine nose for tracking, and he was completely devoted to Johnny. After the first light snow that fall, Johnny and Chum took shortcuts home from school, across the fields, tracking quail and partridge. Chum loved flushing the birds from under the drooping branches of spruce trees and watching them come flapping out to fly off in all directions.

Special privileges came with Johnny's added responsibilities around the farm. His bedtime was extended an hour. He joined the grown-ups by the fire after supper, and listened to his grandfather's stories from the past when he was a hunting guide and trapper. Big

John loved to display his family photographs, yellowed with age. One of the photographs showed him beside his father, a handsome Micmac Indian. Standing straight and tall, smiling broadly, Big John's father was dressed in buckskin and ceremonial headdress for a large family powwow. There were boys and girls of various ages with long, shiny black hair and big, dark eyes. They wore moccasins and beaded headbands, and porcupine quills decorated the sleeves of their garments. Horses without saddles stood in the background. On the back of the photograph, in faded pencil, was written *John Victor Lightfoot 5 years old, 1885*. Another photograph showed Big John, much older but still a young man, shaking hands with two impressive white gentlemen in beaver hats. A large document lay open on a table before them, the deed for the farm that the Lightfoot family would eventually call home.

There was also a photo of a great black bear with a hunter standing nearby. Big John's often-repeated and embellished tale of this dangerous killer bear never failed to stir Johnny's imagination. He'd lie awake for hours, thinking about how exciting and sad it must have been for the hunter to track and bring down such a magnificent beast. It made Johnny feel good to know that many other such bears roamed freely in the north woods.

One evening in October, Billy reported news of a rogue wildcat—a lynx—killing and stealing chickens at night from some of the farmers outside the village.

"Everyone's talking about it at Milligan's Store," Billy said. "George Potts took a shot as it was coming out of his chicken coop, but missed. He said it's a real big one. Cyril said it was more than likely a fox. But George said he got a good look at it in his headlights—short tail, tufted ears, beard, and everything. George lost three of his best laying hens. Ralph Larson's place was raided a couple nights before. The next morning he found a pile of feathers behind his barn. Tom and Jimmy Callahan are tracking it first thing tomorrow morning. Maybe they'll find the cat's lair and trap it, take it west, and release it in the timberlands."

Billy took a swallow of coffee. "I'm going with them," he said.

"Oh, boy!" Johnny shouted, jumping up from the table. "What an adventure! I sure wish I could go." A glance at his father's face dampened his enthusiasm.

After supper that night, Johnny lit his kerosene lamp and carried it upstairs to his room to finish his homework. Distracted by thoughts of the lynx, he read the same paragraph from his history book several times before giving up and blowing out the lamp. He sat on the edge of his bed until his eyes grew accustomed to the darkness. In the distance beyond the barn, the tops of trees stood silhouetted against the Milky Way. A light snow muffled the whisper of a slight breeze through the deep, peaceful woods. Looking up into the sky, he watched tiny crystals of frost sparkle in the starlight, swirling through the air in slow motion.

That magnificent cat is out there somewhere.

Johnny's eyes narrowed on the woods beyond the barn, and his mind drifted into a dream-like state.... *The lynx rises from its lair, yawning widely, the tip of its pink tongue curling backward, teeth sharp, healthy, and white. Its breath hangs on the frosty air. As it stretches its front legs, then the hindquarters, the muscles ripple along its flank. It emerges into the pristine night, slinking noiselessly through the underbrush on heavily padded paws, the fur thick between its toes. The beautiful body is taut, yellow eyes clear, and sharp, tufted ears pointed straight ahead. It stops to listen. There is no movement, no rustling, no flap of owls' wings, no night birds calling. The cat lifts its head, its nostrils quivering.*

It continues its mission, the shoulders rotating slowly around those perfect joints with each step. Nearing its destination, it leaps, lands softly on a log, and crosses a ravine to an open field. Sitting patiently at the edge of the still woods, it sees the lamplight in the windows of a distant house. It lifts its head and licks its thin black lips as it detects the scent of live chickens from Ralph Larson's barn. Crouching low, it will move so stealthily that no dog will bark. It remembers the hole at the bottom of the barn door.

Johnny awoke with a start to the dreamy image of the lynx pouncing on its dinner. Oh, how he wished that he could go tracking with his uncle and the Callahans.

The next day after school, he and Chum cut through Ralph Larson's field. It took them a little out of their way, but Johnny wanted to see those chicken feathers behind Larson's barn. Johnny and Chum picked their way through the stubbly fields, the wind having blown some of the snow off the flatness of it. When they reached the barn, they circled around to the back. Chum sniffed at a spot in a little snowdrift, and dug with his front paws until the soggy feathers flew out between his hind legs. Johnny examined the killing site. The ground was covered with blood. The boy shivered in his jacket. Chum circled the spot, then sniffed all the tracks and circled again. He stopped suddenly and looked off into the distance. He began barking excitedly, and Johnny knew he'd picked up the scent of the lynx. Chum then took off to the north, across the fields, in the direction of the mine, with Johnny right behind him.

Johnny stopped when he reached the big boulder below the outcropping, the site of one of the "secret" paths to the mine. His parents and Billy had forbidden him to go into the mine for "any reason whatsoever." But Chum had found the steep path through the rocks, and he scratched and clawed until he gained a foothold, then scampered to the top of the outcropping. Johnny had never seen him so excited and determined. Chum dashed away over the rocks until he was out of sight. Johnny knew that the dog was smart enough to keep his distance and stay out of trouble should he come upon the lynx. He could still hear Chum barking and hoped the dog wouldn't force the cat so deep into the mine that they couldn't follow.

In spite of his parents' warning, Johnny formulated a plan to trap the lynx. First, he calculated how long it would take him to run home, grab a trap and some bait, and return to the mine. He'd set the trap on the east side of the mine without going in too far. He was positive that the cat was up there and that Chum would flush it out. Uncle Billy could check the trap the next day, and if the cat was in it . . . well, it was just too exciting to think about.

"Keep him there, Chum," Johnny yelled. "I'll be right back."

He ran home, chose one of his father's best traps from the barn, and cut off a sizable chunk of cured bacon hanging from a rafter to use as bait. He was back at the mine in twenty minutes, having taken a shorter path that he had discovered a while back. He followed the sound of Chum's barking until he spotted the dog sniffing and running in circles around the foot of a big pine tree.

Johnny unloaded the gear from his shoulders and started to set out the trap. Then he heard a bloodcurdling snarl.

As he spun around, he spotted the lynx crouched in the tree just a few feet above his head. Ears back and teeth bared, the cat had its yellow-green eyes fastened on him. Chum stiffened and curled back his lips. His hackles bristled the full length of his body, and he growled a warning from deep in his throat. He was ready for a fight. But Johnny's blood ran cold, and his mouth was as dry as cotton. Seconds passed. He desperately wanted to turn and run, but one of Billy's rules of the woods flashed through his head: At close range, never turn your back on a wild animal.

Johnny fought to control the fear that he knew the cat would sense. He stared directly into those hard, cold eyes with all the intensity and courage he could muster. Then, very slowly, he put one foot behind the other, inching himself away from the tree. Without blinking his eyes or moving his lips, he spoke quietly to Chum to come away. Chum stopped growling, although he never took his eyes off the spitting, hissing animal. Johnny walked backward until the cat turned, leaped to a higher limb of the tree, and disappeared among its thick branches.

Only then did he turn and run, with Chum at his heels. But he had gone no more than a few yards when, too late, he saw the edge of an open mine shaft. Dead branches and debris crisscrossed the dark hole. In a split second they gave way under his weight, and he fell through, arms and legs flailing.

He landed face-down twelve feet below on crossbeams that were wedged at an angle into the crumbling walls of the shaft. His impact sent large rocks and other debris splashing into deep water far below. In the semidarkness he raised his head, gasping and coughing, until he caught his breath. He was dazed, but his strong survival instincts took over, and he tried to size up his predicament. He was sure that no bones were broken, but he was afraid that if he tried moving he might dislodge the timbers, plunging him to certain death. He lay there motionless until his heart stopped pounding.

Chum was barking and whining, circling the edge of the hole. Pawing the ground, he sent a shower of snow and gravel down on Johnny; it bounced off him and splashed into the depth below. Johnny called to him, "Chum, no! Help! Go get Uncle Billy, Chum." His voice broke with a sob. "Please, help." Chum barked once, then disappeared from the edge of the shaft.

Johnny carefully turned his body to ease the pressure on his stomach and rib cage. The timbers slipped a couple of inches; he gasped and held his breath. He clutched the beams with both arms and sobbed. He was alone and in greater danger than ever before in his life.

Johnny's head swam with confused images and strange sounds. For a confused moment he thought he was at home in his own bed. It was 5 a.m., still dark, time to get up and begin his chores. He could smell the heat from the kitchen woodstove coming up through his floor grate. Gradually, the image of his falling into the shaft pierced his consciousness, and he remembered what had happened. A shot of panic gripped him, tightening his throat. His body felt stiff and sore. He smelled a strong odor of stagnant water and damp earth. He strained to listen for any sounds—water dripping, a cricket chirping somewhere below, the distant barking of a dog. Where could Chum be? His parents would be sick with worry by his absence at supper. He knew they would be looking for him at this very minute. He had been stupid to disobey his parents and to think he could trap the lynx by himself. He groaned softly in the darkness, realizing that he might never see his family again. He wanted desperately to yell for help, but he was too terrified to move a muscle.

Then, suddenly, he heard a sound from above. He carefully turned his head to listen. Footsteps were slowly approaching the hole. He tried his voice; it sounded like the whimper of a sick puppy. He blinked hard to clear his vision. Maybe it was Mr. Norris, the government man. Whoever it was, Johnny knew that somehow he must get the person's attention. He slowly raised his head and was about to cry out when a dim glow slowly spread over the opening of the hole. Johnny's heart leaped with excitement. His rescuer had built a fire and would save him. Encouraged by that thought, he looked up. But what he saw was the frightening face of Old Maud.

 # Three

Old Maud lay on her stomach at the edge of the hole and lowered a candle in a rusty tin can. Its upward light cast her features in grotesque shadows. Her one pale eye shone huge and round; her left cheekbone cast a darkness deep into a sunken, empty socket. Patches of white hair formed a wispy halo around her twisted face. Johnny tried to scream, but a wave of nausea washed over him and he came close to passing out. His bladder let go, and a warm wetness spread down his legs.

Johnny's glazed eyes followed the candle's descent until Old Maud's face disappeared in the darkness. The candle lodged itself into a crevice just inches from his head.

The shock of seeing Old Maud so close displaced any hope Johnny had of being rescued. In total despair he looked down into the gaping darkness and wondered what kind of death might be worse—disappearing into the void below, or being captured by a sinister witch. He blinked hard again as though it might clear his head. Old Maud had probably seen Chum or heard his barking and come to investigate. Perhaps she wouldn't harm him after all. He wondered whether he could reason with her. Perhaps she was like the hunchback in the story they were reading in school. She had given him a light. Would she go for help? Forcing himself to look up again, he saw an orange glow and a shower of red sparks rising against the blackness of the night sky. He could hear Old Maud moving around the hole. In the distance he again heard a barking dog. He strained to listen. Judging from the light above, Old Maud's fire was a few feet from the opening of the shaft, but now it sounded as though her footsteps were moving away. Then Johnny heard Chum's familiar bark and the voices of several men yelling to one another. He held his breath until his father's voice called his name, and his heart leaped.

"Father! Father, I'm down here! Help! Down here in the shaft!" he shouted excitedly, forgetting his perilous position. Five faces appeared around the edge of the hole—Nathan's, Billy's, the Callahans', and Chum's. Tears of relief welled up in Johnny's eyes. Nathan called down to him. He saw his son clutching the timber in the dim light. He was so relieved to see Johnny that he didn't question the source of the candle. As for the fire, he assumed that Johnny had built it before he fell into the hole.

"Johnny! Are you hurt, Son? Thank heavens we found you. Chum tracked us in the woods and led us into the mine. Then we saw the fire." As he spoke, Nathan quickly judged the danger of the situation. He realized that at any moment the logs upon which Johnny lay might disengage from the sides of the shaft. He removed his shirt and demanded the others do the same. As he was tying the shirts together into a rope and determining the best way for them to reach Johnny, he stepped on a coiled rope lying beside the fire.

"I wonder where this rope came from," said Nathan as he examined it. There was a sophisticated loop tied at one end. He glanced around, but saw no one in the darkness beyond the fire-light. He abandoned the knotted shirts and instead lowered the rope into the shaft.

"Listen carefully, Johnny," Nathan called down. "There's a good, strong knot in this rope. I'm going to lower it down to you. I can see you, Johnny. Open the loop, and put one arm at a time through it. Can you do that? Are you hurt?"

"No, Father, I can do it. I can do it."

"Mind you, don't put the loop over your head first," Nathan

instructed. "Put one arm through and then the other, just like pulling on your undershirt. When you've got your arms through and the rope is snug under both arms, shout. We'll bring you up when you're ready. Do you . . . understand?" Nathan's voice cracked under the strain.

Johnny watched the rope until it reached the timber, then he called up, "I've got it!" He carefully followed his father's instructions, but as he pulled the knot securely around his chest, the timbers shifted another few inches. He froze and held on.

"Hurry, Johnny. Let go of the timbers," Nathan called down. "Don't worry! If they break loose, you'll be all right. We're all tied to the other end of the rope."

With a great, painful lump in his throat, Johnny looked up and called out, "All right, I'm ready."

Chum began to bark into the hole. Tom Callahan called down, "Don't be afraid. We've got a good grip on the rope. We'll have you outta there in no time."

"All right now. Hang on!" Nathan instructed.

Johnny relaxed his grip on the timber and felt himself being lifted. As he swung clear of the beams, he stretched his legs out in front of him, as though aloft on his backyard swing. But as his feet hit the shaft wall, they sent more debris crashing down over the crossbeams. Suddenly, the lower end of the timbers broke away. In seconds, the beams—and the wood and rocks that had held them in place—plunged into the darkness. It sounded like the roll of distant thunder. Johnny's arms and legs went limp as he dangled at the end of the rope. Then he felt himself being lifted again. His body seemed very light, as though he were flying, free from the timbers and his fear.

When he was finally on solid ground, his legs were shaking so much that they would not support his weight. Johnny placed his hands on his knees as though to steady them, and discovered his wet pants. Tears welled in his eyes from embarrassment. Nathan held his son close and whispered, "It's all right, Son. It's all right now."

Billy and the Callahan brothers, joking and singing Irish songs to celebrate Johnny's rescue, took turns carrying him home on their backs. When they arrived, Mary rushed out the door and threw her arms around her son and tearfully covered his face with kisses. Johnny was so happy to see his family, he threw his arms wide around his mother, Big John, and Seth all at once. Nell and Janie hugged his legs and wouldn't let go. They all cried with joy. Then Mary prepared a hot bath for Johnny. Afterward, she applied ointment and bandaged his scrapes and bruises.

When Johnny was safely tucked into bed, his parents, their anger forgotten at his foolhardy behavior, wanted to know everything that had happened. His eyelids heavy with exhaustion, and drifting in and out of sleep, Johnny briefly described his attempt to trap the lynx, how bravely Chum had kept the cat at bay, and how he fell into the shaft. He explained how terribly frightened he was when he saw Old Maud, how he tried to keep his wits about him, and how she built the fire and lowered the candle. Nathan's questions were answered. He knew now that the rope belonged to the old woman, and what she had planned to do with it.

Big John interceded. "Let the boy rest now," he insisted. "There's plenty of time for more questions when he's feeling better."

Later in his room, Big John worried about Johnny's bizarre description of Old Maud. The sight of her distorted face and empty eye socket must have been a terrible shock, and one Johnny would not soon forget. Still, it was obvious that Old Maud's interrupted plan was to rescue him. Big John wondered what was bringing her closer to the village, and if she had anything to do with the lynx raids. Although there had been several distant sightings of her over the years, mostly from hunters in the woods, lately Big John's neighbors had reported seeing her on Cobequid Road, and several times on the tracks. And Herb Norris had been putting out food for her. In spite of Big John's reluctance to believe the superstitious stories about Old Maud, they made him uncomfortable. With some effort, he forced these dark thoughts from his mind.

Johnny slept fitfully that night, with the ugly face of Old Maud and the lynx's eyes swimming through his dreams. He could still see the flickering candle in the rusty tin can as she lowered it to him through the darkness. But he was beginning to realize that, in spite of his fears, Old Maud's fire and the rope she left had been vital to his rescue.

"You're famous, Johnny," Billy exclaimed, bursting into Johnny's room the next day. "At Milligan's Store they're saying you fell thirty feet, just clear of the water, and lived to tell about it."

Johnny chuckled, then winced from his sore stomach muscles.

The excitement died down after a few days—no thanks to the Callahan brothers, who added more details and a longer fall each time the story was told. But the fire near the shaft, the rope, and the candle remained a mystery to everyone except Johnny and his family. At Milligan's Store the gossipers pondered the possibilities. Some good Samaritan, no doubt. But who? In this context, Old Maud's name was never mentioned.

Johnny stayed home from school for a couple of days to settle himself. When Bob and Fisher, his two best friends, brought his homework, they coaxed him to tell them the "real story, straight from the horse's mouth." He told them only the barest facts—mostly about the lynx and what had gone through his mind when he was clinging to the timber. They wanted to know exactly how scared he was, and if he thought he was going to die.

"What if Old Maud had shown up?" Fisher asked. "Boy, you were lucky!" Johnny, flustered at the comment, quickly changed the subject. For reasons he couldn't explain, he didn't tell them about how Old Maud helped him. They wouldn't have believed him anyway. He felt resentful and angry when his friends had referred to her as "the witch." He decided to speak to his father and Billy about his mixed and troubled thoughts.

Four

Life on the farm returned to normal. Johnny went back to school, and the Lightfoot household prepared for the long winter months ahead. On Saturdays, he helped his uncle and his father haul their firewood on the heavy wagon pulled by the big dray horses. They had cut the wood the year before and left it to season in a clearing in the forest. On the first logging day, Chum flushed partridge and quail from under the low branches of a pine tree a little way off the trail. The dog looked over his shoulder to see if the men were watching. Johnny laughed, and called him back, "Not yet, Chum. It's too early in the season for hunting. Come on, fella."

One of Johnny's new responsibilities was accompanying Nathan and Billy on their annual trip to the fishermen's market in Musquodoboit, where they bought fresh herring. They would then salt it down and pack it in barrels and store it in the barn. The salt herring provided one of the family's food staples during the winter. The fish was boiled and served with red potatoes and strips of fried lean pork. They also bought large fillets of dry codfish and hung them on wire stretched between the barn walls, away from field mice and other small animals. Molasses was stored in its special barrel with a spigot at the bottom; the barrel fit snugly in its little cradle near the barn door. The kerosene was stored at a safe distance from the barn, in a similar but much larger barrel. The barn was Johnny's favorite place, and he never complained about his chores there. He loved the scent of apples carefully stored in baskets inside the barn, the sweet-smelling bales of hay stored in the loft, and the warm body smell of the animals. He also helped his father overhaul the snares and traps for the upcoming hunting season, and helped stack firewood high against the north wall of the chicken coop.

His mother and the younger children put up peaches and apples, and made pickles, grape jelly, relishes, and tomato sauce to add to the larder of berries and vegetables that they had preserved earlier. Although Mary stored many of the jars in the root cellar, she liked to keep the more colorful ones on the kitchen shelf that had been built to display them. During these preparations, the house was filled with warmth and delightful smells.

The Lightfoot family talked among themselves and with their neighbors about the coming winter. Big John, examining a woolly-bear caterpillar, reported, "The fur on the caterpillars and the squirrels, too, is thick this year. I think we'll have a cold winter with lots of snow." Cyril and old Mr. Callahan observed that the deer and moose populations were bigger than ever. There was a difference of opinion as to how long into the winter the waterfowl might stay. Almost everyone agreed on how much snow was expected from the signs of food-gathering by the smaller "varmints."

Billy and the Callahans had long ago stopped tracking the rogue lynx. What tracks there were had been washed away by the rain a day or two after Johnny's accident in the mine. There had been no new reports of killed chickens or raided barns, so everyone assumed that the cat had returned to its wilderness habitat.

As fall deepened and winter approached, Johnny found himself thinking about Old Maud. He wanted her to know how thankful he was for her help in his rescue. Sympathy and gratitude began to replace the fear and revulsion he had felt for Old Maud in the beginning. She had given him the light, and he felt strongly about wanting to thank her.

~ ~ ~

One Saturday evening in late November, the Lightfoot men had just finished dinner. A heavy snow had fallen earlier, and they had cleared paths to the barn, the well, and the road. They were tired but in good spirits, smoking their pipes, telling stories, and drinking coffee in front of the fire. Chum lay near the hearth, his chin resting on his front paws, eyes blinking sleepily. Out of the corner of his eye, Johnny saw Chum suddenly raise his head and cock his ears. The dog sprang to his feet and shot to the kitchen door, then stood motionless, ears strained forward. The hackles rose on his neck. A long, low growl rumbled in his chest and erupted from his throat.

"Listen!" cautioned Big John. "Mary, keep the children quiet," he whispered. Seconds passed.

"It's coming from the barn," said Nathan. "Something's after the livestock!"

Billy and Nathan snatched their guns from the wall and ran out the door, with Chum dashing ahead of them. Through the porch window, Johnny saw Chum squeeze through the jagged hole in the bottom of the barn door. Johnny and Big John caught up to the others just as they heard the bone-chilling snarls of two animals locked in combat. Defending his territory, Chum had taken on whatever wild animal he had found in the barn.

Billy's chestnut mare, Ruby, reared in her stall as the men threw open the barn door. The cows bellowed and broke their tethers. Big John quickly slammed the door shut to stop them from escaping the barn. In a flurry of feathers, the chickens flew as a flock to the rafters, their wings outstretched for balance. The snarling sounds suddenly stopped. At first, Johnny thought that whatever Chum had attacked either escaped or had been killed. He called to his dog. When Chum didn't come, he looked for him among the shuffling feet of the cows while Nathan and Billy tried to calm the wild-eyed Ruby. In desperation, Johnny ran in and out of each stall, then around to the hayloft.

There, at the foot of the ladder, Chum lay in a motionless heap covered with blood. As Johnny approached, he raised his head from the bloody floorboards and whimpered softly. Johnny knelt beside him and held the lantern high. Horrified, he saw that Chum's underbelly and throat had been badly mauled.

A wave of nausea rolled inside Johnny's stomach as he cried out to his father. Then he caught a sudden movement above him in the loft, followed by a low guttural sound. Particles of hay filtered down through the cracks of the floor. He looked up and saw the familiar yellow eyes and the needle-sharp teeth of the lynx. He quickly got to his feet and extended his arms as though to meet the challenge of the threatening animal. As it sprang from the edge of the loft, Johnny heard a shot ring out. The cat fell dead at his feet. Billy was a good shot.

Big John glanced from the dead lynx to Chum's bloody belly, and put an arm around his grandson's shoulders. Johnny watched in shock while his father and Billy carefully examined the dog. Nathan ripped off both sleeves of his shirt and bandaged Chum's middle as best he could, while Billy held his neckerchief against the dog's bleeding throat.

Billy stood up and shook his head. "Chum is in bad shape. He's all chewed up. I don't think he'll last the night."

Johnny's hands began to tremble; his legs nearly gave way. He couldn't speak.

"You know what has to be done, Son," said Nathan.

"I'm sorry, Johnny," said Big John softly, and left the barn.

Johnny knelt and looked into Chum's eyes. He was suffering, there was no doubt. He touched the dog's head. Chum had been his friend like no other, so stout of heart, so brave. He couldn't believe or accept what had happened in the last few minutes. Johnny looked at Chum's mutilated body as though his love for the dog could restore its vitality.

"Father," he pleaded, "please don't. Let me stay here in the barn with him tonight. In the morning, if he's no better, I'll come for you, I promise."

Reluctantly, Nathan agreed. Billy just shook his head. Letting an animal suffer was contrary to the family's spiritual convictions.

"I'll bring you one of your grandfather's pain poultices," Billy said quietly. "It'll help stop the bleeding, too, and keep the fever down."

A few minutes later Billy returned with the poultice, some blankets, a bucket of warm water, a bottle of drinking water, and a fresh lantern. Johnny cleaned Chum's wounds with the warm water, applied the poultice, then covered the dog with one of the blankets. Billy watched with a heavy heart. He wanted to say something but decided against it. Silently, he bundled the body of the lynx into a burlap sack and left.

Johnny settled himself close to Chum to keep him warm. After an hour the dog seemed to rest, but Johnny was not consoled. He cradled Chum's head in his arms and spoke softly to him.

"Don't die, Chum," he pleaded. "I can't let you die. You've got to trust me, boy."

He rocked Chum's body in his arms. Tears rolled down his face and fell on Chum's bloody head. Johnny knew that the dog's chances for survival were hopeless if he didn't take drastic measures immediately. The idea had been in the back of his mind all along: Old Maud would have some strong medicine, even stronger than his grandfather's poultice. She had helped him before. Maybe she could help save his dog's life. She was his only hope.

Johnny moved slowly away from the dog without disturbing him. He took down his sturdy sled from the barn wall. He gently wrapped Chum in a couple of the blankets, carefully loaded him onto the sled, and tied him in place so he couldn't roll off. He dribbled some water into Chum's mouth, then took a swig from the bottle. After checking the lantern's supply of kerosene, and bundling up an extra blanket and some makings for a fire, he set out for the mine to find Old Maud.

Five

It was past midnight when Johnny left the barn. The night was cold, and a foot of snow lay on the ground. In a half hour he had crossed the railroad tracks at Cobequid Road and found the familiar path to the mine marked by an old tree that had been struck by lightning. He climbed the embankment, carefully pulling the sled behind him. Chum whimpered, and Johnny checked to make sure that the dog was still secure on the sled. The moon was very bright, and Johnny had no trouble finding the spot where he had fallen into the mine shaft. The hole was now staked and covered with heavy planks under the snow, because Herb Norris had sent a letter to his superiors demanding that they "reseal all vertical shafts," and cited Johnny Lightfoot's recent accident.

At a safe distance from the edge of the shaft, Johnny built a fire with the wood he had brought, then wrapped himself in the extra blanket. He sat beside Chum's sled, confident that Old Maud would come. He fought to stay awake, but exhaustion overcame him, and he dozed off almost immediately.

He suddenly awoke to find Old Maud bent over Chum, examining his wounds. The sky had lightened in the east; the fire was only a bed of dull coals. Johnny rubbed his eyes and gazed at Old Maud. She wore a long robe of animal skins with a loose hood covering her white hair, and fur boots held together with thin strips of hide. In the light of her lantern, she looked like a great brown bear. Johnny stiffened when she peered at him from the shadow of the hood.

"Bring the dog—follow me," she said.

The sound of her voice so shocked Johnny that for a second he thought that someone else had spoken. Her voice was deep, almost like a man's, and hesitant, as though she hadn't spoken aloud for some time. But the tone was clear. Johnny picked up the sled's rope and followed a few yards behind Old Maud. He was scared, but his fear for Chum's life gave him courage. He kept her in sight as she rounded rocky outcroppings and wove among clumps of bushes. Recalling the rumors, Johnny wondered whether she would change into a dreadful beast before his very eyes. He was surprised at her agility; she didn't rest or seem to be hampered by the deep snow.

After several minutes, she stopped at the mouth of a horizontal mine shaft, like a sloping tunnel, between two massive boulders. She looked over her shoulder and motioned for Johnny to follow. He stopped and watched as she entered a few feet into the darkness. Her lantern, swaying as she walked, sent her shadow looming back and forth, short and tall, onto the immense vertical rock walls on either side. To his amazement, the lamplight suddenly shot through the top of the cave. It had no roof. The shadows stopped dancing. Old Maud was waiting.

Johnny dreaded what he might see if he went through the opening, not to mention what might happen to him and his dog should rumors about Old Maud prove to be true. He looked behind him at his own deep footprints between the tracks of the sled runners, and longed for the safe place he had come from. Then his eyes fell on Chum, who whimpered on the sled. He tightened his grip on the rope and stepped through the gaping entrance.

Johnny could have sworn he saw a crooked little smile at the corner of Old Maud's twisted mouth as he came into her pool of light.

She turned and walked a few more yards along the narrow path. Beyond the glow of her lantern, Johnny saw a flicker of light. As they came closer, he saw a candle set in a window of a small cabin. Even in the dim light, he could see that it was constructed of stout logs and was wedged between two great rocks with barely enough space on either side for a person to squeeze through. A tin roof extended about two feet over the wooden door. In the darkness, he couldn't see what was behind the cabin.

This is the witch's den! he thought.

Old Maud lifted the latch and opened the door. Somewhere from inside came a sound like that of a squawking bird. Without turning, she said, "Bring the dog." With his heart beating hard against his ribs, Johnny carefully lifted Chum from the sled and carried him into the cabin. He knew now that there was no turning back.

It was dark inside except for the candle in the window. Old Maud shrugged off her robe into a corner, then fed a few pieces of wood to the glowing embers in a potbellied stove. The flames threw more light into the room, casting a gigantic shadow of Old Maud as she moved around the cabin. From its perch somewhere above Johnny's head, a large crow descended and landed heavily on the rough floorboards. The firelight glistened on its blue-black feathers as it strutted toward the light.

"Put the dog there," she ordered, pointing to an animal skin on the floor near the stove. Johnny did as he was told, while Old Maud set about lighting two more candles with a long splinter of wood. He stealthily glanced around the room while he stroked Chum's ears, hoping that Old Maud wouldn't hear the thumping of his own heart.

The only furniture in the cabin was a heavily scarred rectangular table, an old rocking chair, and a stool made from birch branches. A wooden shelf behind the stove held some battered tin pots, kettles, and bottles of various sizes. Fragrant bunches of herbs, roots, and dried apples were strung from the rafters. A freshly skinned rabbit and two dressed-out partridges hung from wooden pegs. On the wall opposite the front door, another door stood partially open. The only window in the main room was the one that had held the lighted candle, which Old Maud had moved and placed on the table beside the other two. The extra light made the cabin seem less formidable. Johnny relaxed a little as he watched Old Maud prepare to administer to Chum.

She took a wire-handled tin kettle from the shelf and disappeared through the partially open door. In seconds, she reappeared with strips of clean white cloth and the kettle full of water, which she placed on the woodstove. She took down a small glass bottle from the shelf, removed the cork, and poured some of the clear liquid into the water. Then she plucked a few dried blossoms from a bunch of twigs, added them to the brew, and stirred it with a wooden spoon.

As though suddenly remembering that Johnny was still there, she looked at him, then at Chum. In a quiet and oddly comforting voice, she said, "Maud will cure your dog. In seven nights, come alone to the same place."

His eyes downcast, Johnny knelt on the floor beside Chum, cradling the dog's head in his lap. He didn't know exactly how to tell Maud what was in his heart. It was important that she believe his words, but to convey his sincerity and respect, he must look at her directly, as his father had taught him. He turned, looked fully into her face, and spoke with tears in his eyes.

"Thank you," he whispered. "I hope . . . I mean, I know . . . you can save him. And thank you for the . . . uh . . . light in the shaft."

Quickly lowering his eyes, he said to Chum, "Don't you worry, boy. You'll be all right now. Just do what you're told and I'll be back in a few days."

He kissed Chum between the ears and got to his feet. At the door he turned to see Old Maud applying her medicine to the dog's underbelly. Johnny closed the door behind him. Hoping he had made the right decision, he headed home with a heavy heart.

 *Six*

At 4:00 a.m. Nathan awoke with a start, jumped out of bed, and ran to the window. He looked toward the barn. There was no light in the barn window facing the house. He decided not to wake Mary. He pulled on his pants and shirt and went quietly downstairs. He started making the fire in the stove, but something nagged at him to put off lighting it until he checked on Johnny and Chum. He pulled on a sheepskin jacket and boots and lit a lantern, then silently closed the kitchen door behind him so as not to awaken his family before it was time for chores. In the bitter cold, the snow crunched and squeaked under his boots as he made his way to the barn.

He opened the small side door and shined his lantern inside. As he called out, the animals shuffled and murmured. His light fell on the bloody spot where Chum had lain. The first feelings of apprehension wormed their way into his stomach. When his worst fears were confirmed, Nathan rushed back to the house and checked Johnny's room, then he woke his brother.

"Billy, Johnny and the dog aren't in the barn, and they're not in his room," Nathan exclaimed. "Could he have—?"

Billy bolted upright in his bed. "I suspected this," he said, throwing off the covers. "He's taken the dog to Old Maud."

~ ~ ~

When Johnny arrived home, it was full daylight. His father and Billy were waiting for him in the barn. Nathan's face was stern.

"Where have you been, Johnny? And where is the dog?" he demanded.

Johnny took a deep breath. "I've been in the mine, Father. I took Chum there last night to find Old Maud. I lit a fire and she found us. Chum is with her now, and she's going to make him well."

"I knew it!" said Billy.

Nathan pursed his lips and sighed. "Johnny, Johnny," he said, shaking his head. "I forbade you to go into the mine. It's very hard for me to believe that you disobeyed me *again*. As for Old Maud, I doubt she can cure Chum—unless, of course, she really is a witch. His wounds are much too serious."

"And what if she *is* a witch," Johnny retorted. "With her powers she can cure him if anyone can. I had to go, Father. And I'm supposed to go back for him in a week."

"You will do nothing of the kind," Nathan sputtered in anger. "Do you know what you've done? You've defied the tradition of our forefathers who taught us that we are all brothers, man and beast, and that we must protect and honor all living things. You've prolonged the suffering of a hopelessly wounded animal. For that you'll be punished, Johnny, and punished severely. Your own conscience will punish you even more." Nathan took a deep breath. "We'll discuss this further after supper tonight. Now, get ready for school, and ask your mother's forgiveness for the anguish you've caused her this morning."

All day at school Johnny couldn't concentrate on his work. He was worried—not just because of his impending punishment but because his father had planted a seed of further doubt in his mind. What if Old Maud's treatments don't work? How long will she let Chum suffer before she puts him out of his misery? And with some poison potion, no doubt. And how will he learn the fate of his poor dog if he can't go back to the mine? These questions burned in his mind. What a fool he was to believe that Old Maud could save Chum's life.

That evening at supper the family was very quiet. Mary's attempts at various topics of light conversation to ease the tension failed miserably.

As soon as supper was over, Nathan announced to Johnny, "Your Uncle Billy and I will see you in your room. Now."

Whenever his uncle's presence was required, Johnny knew that Billy and his father had already discussed the issue. Although he was nervous, he felt encouraged, because Uncle Billy had always been his ally under such circumstances. Of course, Billy would never openly challenge Nathan—his older brother, the elder son— but Johnny knew that his uncle would help him argue his case.

Mary excused Johnny from the table with a concerned glance at her husband. The sympathetic eyes of the younger children and Big John followed Johnny away from the table. He went to his room and waited. A few minutes later Nathan knocked; he and Billy entered, then closed the door behind them. Nathan sat on the bed beside Johnny while Billy straddled the wooden chair by the window.

Nathan began. "I want you to know that I understand what Chum means to you, and that saving his life was uppermost in your mind. It took a lot of courage to face the dangers of the mine alone at night, to actually *go looking* for Old Maud. Her reputation for witchcraft has circulated through this county longer than I can remember. You are a brave young man. But you're also foolhardy and stubborn."

Johnny began to speak. Nathan interrupted, "No, let me finish. You'll get your chance. You were wrong to go without permission and alone, but had I followed my own instincts, my own judgment, we would not be having this discussion. I'm partly to blame. We were sick with worry when we discovered that you were gone. I wanted to track you at four o'clock this morning, but Billy talked me into waiting. He guessed right away where you had gone. Billy doesn't believe in witches. He believes that Old Maud is a Micmac medicine woman." He looked at Billy and smiled.

The tension was relieved. Johnny asked if he could explain his recent feelings about Old Maud. Nathan nodded yes.

"I wanted to tell you this before, Father," Johnny said. "I never *really* believed that Old Maud was a witch. At least, not since my fall into the shaft. Although, when I was following her to her cabin last night, I couldn't help thinking about what I had heard at Milligan's Store. I was plenty scared, afraid she might turn herself into some kind of horrible creature, and Chum and I would be goners, but it didn't happen."

Then he described his second encounter with Old Maud. Nathan wanted to know the exact whereabouts of Old Maud's cabin, but Johnny explained why he couldn't tell. He repeated Old Maud's instruction that he come *alone* in seven nights.

Nathan strongly objected to that idea. Johnny started to protest when Billy interrupted.

"I can understand your concern, Nathan, but we have to know what's happened to the dog. We could easily track the way to Old Maud's cabin, but she's trusting Johnny to come alone. She's probably treating Chum with herbs and roots like Father uses in his poultices and tonics. We have to find out if Chum is dead or alive. I don't think Johnny is in any real danger if he follows his own tracks from last night. There will be no big snow while the moon is waning. And from what Johnny's told us, I think he has a new and different kind of respect for Old Maud."

"Please, Father," Johnny begged. "Uncle Billy is right. I'm thirteen years old, and I'm not afraid anymore. Old Maud won't hurt me. I'm sure of that. She gave me a light and built that fire. I'll be very careful. You can wait up for me, and if I'm not home by midnight, you and Uncle Billy can follow my tracks right to Old Maud's cabin."

Nathan sat silently stroking his beard, mulling over Johnny's words. His decision would not come easily. "I'll decide in three days," Nathan said, then he got up and left the room. Billy followed, but as he closed Johnny's bedroom door, he smiled, winked, and nodded his head encouragingly.

Johnny wasn't completely sure of his father's consent, but if his decision was favorable, he must be prepared for his return to the mine. He made several trips to the barn, checked and rechecked the kerosene in the biggest lantern, and carefully trimmed the wick. Then he bundled some firewood in birch bark, tied it to the sled, and hid the whole thing in an empty stall at the back of the barn. He put a small box of matches into his jacket pocket; then, feeling nervous about someone finding them there and asking questions, he removed them and placed them in the mouse-proof matchbox over the barn door.

On the third evening after their discussion, Johnny paced his room until he was called down for supper. He sat in his usual place at the table, on his father's left. He couldn't read his father's face. Mary, on Nathan's right, silently served meat onto their plates. Big John, at the other end of the table, cast his eyes from face to face. Billy and the children quietly passed the vegetables and kept their eyes on Mary. Johnny studied his mother's expression, but it told him nothing until she passed his plate to him. Then she looked directly into his eyes and smiled.

He could hardly contain his joy. He returned his mother's smile and quietly thanked his father. The mood suddenly changed, and everyone began talking at once.

Nathan raised his hand for silence and spoke in a grave voice.

"I want you all to remember that Johnny disobeyed the rules." Johnny hung his head. "He had been forbidden to go into the mine. Furthermore, I'm not sure but that he has caused Chum to suffer needlessly. For Johnny's sake, I hope a miracle brings Chum back to us. But there is still the matter of an appropriate punishment. I have given this a great deal of thought. Johnny will clean out three of our neighbors' barns free of charge. In three more days, he'll go, *with* our permission, into the mine to bring back his dog—that is, of course, if Chum is still alive."

Johnny breathed a sigh of relief and again thanked his father. Nathan put his huge, rough hand on Johnny's shoulder. "I won't rest until this terrible ordeal is over."

At last the seven days had passed. Johnny, Billy, and Big John waited in the barn until the waning moon rose over the hill across Loon Lake. They waited for Nathan to come to give his blessing. The sled was ready, the lantern was lighted, and the matches were back in Johnny's pocket. Nathan opened the barn door and stood a few seconds, silhouetted against the sparkling blue-white moonlit snow beyond the doorway. He watched the other men for a moment, listening to Big John's and Billy's advice to Johnny, who was clearly anxious to be off.

"I hope I won't regret this night," said Nathan. "I still think that one of us should follow at a distance behind you."

"Please don't do that, Father!" Johnny exclaimed. "You promised to wait until midnight."

Nathan reached out and hugged his son. "I'll be waiting. The Great Spirit be with you," he said.

Seven

The temperature had dropped sharply since suppertime. Johnny's breath frosted the lock of hair that fell from under his fur-trimmed parka. Each time he inhaled the cold air, the tiny hairs of his nostrils stiffened and stuck together. He followed his week-old tracks to the blackened circle of his previous fire. He was building another among the cinders when he heard footsteps creaking in the snow. He turned quickly to see Old Maud, a few yards away, beckoning him to follow. Chum wasn't with her. Johnny's heart sank. "He must be dead," he said with a groan.

It was true, then. He had foolishly expected Old Maud to perform miracles. He had hoped to see Chum at her side, bounding through the snow, happy to be going home. His father was right. Chum's wounds were much too serious. Hot tears stung his eyes. His legs turned to lead, refusing to move him forward. Why should he go with her now? What was the point, except to bring Chum's body home? Heavy hearted, Johnny followed, grieving, to the cabin at the end of the narrow canyon.

As soon as he set foot on the doorstep, Chum barked from inside. Johnny turned to Old Maud, his grief-stricken face suddenly beaming and his eyes shining with wonder and gratitude.

45

Maud pushed open the door and stood aside. In the warm candlelight, Chum lay on the animal skins in the corner, the crow standing close by. The dog's middle was bound in strips of white cloth. He struggled to his feet as Johnny rushed to his side. Big, happy tears rolled down Johnny's cheeks. He sank to his knees, cradling Chum's head in his arms. He spoke softly to the dog, and Chum licked his wet face. Then suddenly he felt himself being lifted to his feet. Old Maud had an arm around his shoulders. He almost stiffened at her touch, but caught himself—he hoped before she noticed. He allowed himself to be led to the potbellied stove.

"He is no longer in danger," Maud said. "He heals very fast, like the courageous dog he is. Three more days, and you can take him home. Come, have some tea." She pointed to the low stool in front of the stove. Johnny sat down, still careful not to look at Old Maud's face.

She set about heating water in a kettle, and dropped some dry green leaves and a few small twigs into the water as it boiled. When she handed him a tin cup filled with the brew, Johnny hesitated a second before he took it from her. He didn't want to touch her dark, gnarled hands, the skin tight and shiny over the swollen knuckles, the nails ridged and ragged. He watched cautiously as she poured some of the hot liquid into her own cup and drank it. Then he took a sip from his. Not only was it delicious, it soothed and warmed his insides and put him at ease. He was truly no longer afraid, but relaxed and comfortable.

Old Maud reached for a small wooden box with a sliding lid. She pulled out a discolored corncob pipe. From a soft deerskin pouch she filled the pipe with tobacco and lit it with a candle, drawing the yellow flame deep into the dark bowl. Johnny watched her smoke her pipe and drink her tea, the crow perched on her shoulder. She seemed to be in deep thought. Moments passed. Johnny couldn't hold back any longer and blurted out, "How did you do it? What did you give him?"

She slowly raised her head and looked at him. "Herbs. Ointments of my own making. Broth made from the feet of fowl. I fed him by hand. He was very weak. Lost much blood. You must take care that he rests for many days. Feed him well. I will give you a powder to put in his food. Soon he will be as strong as ever."

They sat drinking their tea, with Chum sleeping comfortably in the corner. The crow flew to its shelf behind the stove, and pecked at something in a tin cup.

"My name is Johnny Lightfoot," he began, "and I live on the Lightfoot farm on Cobequid Road. I have—"

"I know who you are," she interrupted calmly, "and I know where you live."

The hair rose on the back of Johnny's neck. What else did she know about him and his family?

"How do you know?" he ventured.

"This county has been my home for many years. My people were the first to settle this valley. I am Micmac," she announced proudly.

Johnny was astonished. With intense interest, he searched her face for characteristic signs that would normally mark her heritage. Whatever had disfigured her face had destroyed the fine Micmac features, except for the high cheekbones. Her lips were unnaturally thin and stretched to one side, grotesquely attached to the shiny scars of her left cheek, exposing her teeth on that side. Wisps of white hair clung to her scalp in patches. And her eye—that large, intense eye—was as *blue* as the summer sky. She withdrew from his gaze. Johnny dropped his eyes, and finished his tea in silence.

"You must leave now," Old Maud said, rising from her chair. "The wind has risen; it is bitter cold. I will walk with you to the shaft. In three days the moon will be in its last quarter. Come then and take your dog home. He will be ready."

Johnny said his farewells to Chum, stroking his ears. "I'll be back soon to take you home." Chum wagged his tail.

Johnny followed Old Maud back to their meeting place. As he turned to go, he said, "My family will be so happy with this good news. They'll be waiting up for me. We all thank you."

Maud nodded and smiled slightly, then turned and headed back to her little house. Johnny climbed down to the lower level of the mine, to the narrow, snowy path that led to the road. He saw a dark figure standing in the path. Billy was waiting for him.

"I thought you might be early," he said, "so I came to meet you."

"It's all right," Johnny said with a smile. "Chum is alive, and he's going to be fine. Old Maud is taking good care of him." Billy beamed and put his arm around Johnny's shoulder. They walked a short distance in silence, each engrossed in his own thoughts about Old Maud and Chum.

"Isn't it strange?" Johnny said at last. "It doesn't matter to Chum what Old Maud looks like. Why is that, Uncle Billy? I was scared to look at her face, just like everybody else around here, but Chum took right to her. Old Maud keeps a big crow, too. It sits on her shoulder."

"Most animals know what's in a person's heart, Johnny. They know when they can trust someone, when someone wants to help. Cruelty is the only ugliness they know."

Johnny's parents and his grandfather were waiting up with a fire burning brightly on the hearth. When he told them about Chum's remarkable recovery, they seemed astounded. "A miracle," they said. They wanted to hear everything that had happened at Old Maud's cabin.

Before he went to sleep that night, Johnny contemplated his Uncle Billy's words about trust. He gave thanks that Old Maud had saved Chum's life—and his, too, for that matter—and for the better feelings he had about Old Maud.

Eight

The next few days seemed endless, but Johnny's heart was filled with joyful anticipation. Two of his neighbors, Mr. Sanders and Mr. Tessier, seemed puzzled but willing to accept Johnny's offer to clean their barns on the following Saturday to fulfill his punishment. He welcomed the hard work and thought the punishment was fair. It would help the time pass until he could return to the mine to bring Chum home. His friends Bob and Fisher went along to give him moral support. Georgie Sanders and Dave Tessier watched and poked fun while Johnny did Georgie's barn chores for the day. Fisher offered his help and nearly came to blows with the hecklers. Although he was annoyed by the jeering, Johnny kept his good humor and insisted on doing the work himself.

Returning from exercising her Uncle Mike's horse, Georgie's cousin Silky Ann Sanders heard the hoots and catcalls and immediately sized up the situation. Silky was twelve, and Georgie thought she was too bossy for a girl. He usually kept his distance when she and her family came to visit.

Silky quickly dismounted, slapped the horse's rump, and sent him into his stall. "Georgie Sanders, you lazy lout. You ought to be ashamed of yourself. Too lazy to do your own chores. Uncle Mike's too easy on you. Hiring Johnny to clean the barn!" She swung angrily around to face Dave. "And what are *you* doing here? Go on home where you belong."

Dave slunk over to the barn door and turned. He didn't want Georgie to think Silky could send him packing.

She approached Johnny, and her voice softened. "You hired yourself out? Why?"

Before he could answer, Georgie piped up. "He ain't hired. He's doin' it for free—as punishment for somethin'. Ain't it, Johnny?"

"I'm not talking to you, Georgie," Silky snapped. "Johnny can speak for himself."

"He's right," Johnny stopped pitching hay to look at her. He was always glad for an excuse to talk to Silky. He thought she was pretty, and he certainly admired her spunk. "I disobeyed my father, and this is my punishment."

"And what did you do that was so bad?"

"I'd rather not say," Johnny threw more hay into a stall.

"Maybe he wet the bed," Georgie snickered. Dave let out a yowl of laughter from the barn door.

Silky whirled around, her eyes fierce with anger. "You shut your mouth, Georgie Sanders. If you had half the decent upbringing like Johnny Lightfoot, I wouldn't be so ashamed of you." She turned on Dave and pointed a commanding finger, "I told *you* to go home. Now *go!*" She took two steps in Dave's direction. He ran from the barn, mumbling something under his breath.

"Yay, Silky!" Bob and Fisher yelled. Johnny was so impressed that he handed his pitchfork to Silky, who laughed and drove the tines into a bale of hay. Bob and Fisher started mucking out two of the stalls. Georgie eventually became bored and sauntered back to the house.

The four of them cleaned Mr. Tessier's barn in much less time without Dave's supervision. It was almost dark when they finished. Johnny thanked Silky, who held out her hand for him to shake. Bob and Fisher walked her back to her Uncle Mike's house and thanked her for helping them.

~ ~ ~

The following Monday after school, Johnny's friends asked him why Chum wasn't waiting outside the schoolhouse, as was his habit. Johnny didn't want to talk about it, but realized that they wouldn't leave him alone until he gave them some kind of an explanation.

He launched into the account of the night the lynx raided his barn and got so caught up in his own tale that, halfway through, he waxed dramatic and started acting out the highlights. He told how Chum had been attacked in the family barn by the notorious lynx, and how he himself had narrowly escaped. He enhanced the lynx's size and ferocity, Chum's incredible bravery, and his Uncle Billy's extraordinary marksmanship.

His friends were so thrilled that he was obliged to repeat it twice, adding a few more details each time to increase the suspense. At the end, Johnny added casually, "Chum was scratched up a bit in the attack, and he's at home recuperating. He'll be all right in a couple of days."

Chum was an instant hero. The story spread from school to Milligan's Store and throughout the village.

The day of the moon's fourth quarter finally arrived. Johnny was much less apprehensive about this trip into the mine. As a token of the family's appreciation, Mary had prepared some gifts for Maud—a dressed chicken wrapped in butcher's paper, and a tinned corn cake. Johnny wrapped them carefully in a brand new blanket, his special gift for Maud, and tied them to his sled.

His climb to the top of the mine seemed shorter and much less strenuous this time. He met Maud at their appointed place, and they walked together to the cabin. Happy to see Johnny, Chum seemed to have some of his old energy back. Apparently knowing he was going home, he chased his tail around the cabin. Maud had removed most of the bandages. Chum still limped a bit, but he barked and snorted with excitement. Maud busied herself poking the fire in the stove and preparing the medicines for Chum's continued treatment.

Johnny looked around the now-familiar room, not quite ready to end his visit. He was astonished by an even greater change in his attitude toward Maud. He actually wanted them to be friends. Although he felt sorry for her, he also felt great admiration and respect.

His thoughts were interrupted when Maud handed him a carefully folded square of brown paper containing a white powder, and a corked bottle filled with brown seeds and green berries. "You must boil a quart of water, and add all of these to it. Steep this mixture until the seeds and berries settle to the bottom of the kettle. Give Chum a tablespoon full of the elixir—no more—in his drinking water every day. A little will go a long way. And sprinkle a pinch of this powder in his food. By the next full moon, you will see that he is stronger, and his coat will be glossy and his eyes will shine." She patted Chum's head. "Fine dog."

Still reluctant to leave, Johnny was glad to have a reason to delay his departure, and he chose that moment to present her with the gifts. "From my mother," he said as he unwrapped the bundle for Maud. "And this is from me," he explained as he unfolded the blanket.

She looked first at the chicken, then at him with a puzzled expression. He knew she was touched. To break the awkward silence, he asked, "Could we have tea before I go?"

She looked at him until the good corner of her mouth rose slightly.

"Then please fetch some water," she said, handing him the kettle. "Through that door and out the next is the well." He smiled back as he went through the door and into the tiny back room.

As subtly as possible, Johnny looked around the room as he passed through it. In the dim light from a tiny window, he saw a platform in one corner with a straw mattress covered with animal skins. Next to that, on a square wooden box, sat a candle and a large book with a badly stained binding. A couple of tin tea boxes—one large, the other small—were the only other furnishings in the room.

He crossed the room to a narrow door with a covered peephole, then drew back the bolt and opened the door. In the fading light he could barely make out a courtyard; it was long and in the center stood a small covered stone well with a crank handle. Large bundles of firewood stood against the back of the house. Oddly, not as much snow lay inside Maud's tidy compound as outside of it. Around the edges of this courtyard were the winter-killed remains of a vegetable and flower garden. On three sides, the sheer rock walls rose at least thirty feet above the cabin. Cleverly concealed from the front and the back, the courtyard had no entrance or exit except through the cabin.

About halfway up the rock walls was a horizontal scar, as though there had been a ceiling over the courtyard. Johnny guessed that this had once been a tunnel whose ceiling had caved in, and the loose rock had been excavated to form this narrow canyon. The courtyard provided excellent protection from the elements, and prevented detection from the occasional passerby on the other side of the rock walls. He decided he would ask Maud about her perfect hideout. He cranked up the water from the well and returned to the cabin, where she was waiting.

He held his questions until they had their tea in hand. She seemed to expect him to speak.

"Why is there so little snow behind your house?" he asked.

"I don't know for sure. The exposure at the top is perfectly due south, and I think the wind blows the snow beyond the opening above the canyon. It is a narrow crevice, unlike some of the others in the mine."

"But the cabin. Who . . . how did you . . . ?" he stammered.

"Many years ago, after the mine closed but before it was sealed, I found this cabin on the north side. It was an abandoned assayer's shack. My kinsman from the next valley brought his oxen, and we took apart the shack and rebuilt it where it is now. It took many days."

"But why do you live in the mine? It's against the law to—" He regretted the words the moment they crossed his lips. "Isn't it?" he quickly added. "How do you manage, all alone?"

"I suppose it *is* against the law, but no one troubles me here. Herb Norris and I have an unspoken understanding. I've lived in this cabin for a very long time. I am self-sufficient, and my needs are few."

"But why don't you live in the village among your own people? There are many Micmacs in our village." There was a long pause before she answered.

"I frighten the children," she said, and peered into the depths of her cup. The many stories about "Old Maud" ran through Johnny's mind, and he felt thoroughly ashamed.

"But that's because they don't know you. Why, when everyone finds out how you saved my dog's life and how kind—"

"No!" The tone of her voice startled him. Seeing alarm on his face, she said in a softer voice, "No one must know about that except your own family."

She rose and went into the next room, and closed the door behind her. Johnny was perplexed. He thought he offended her, and shame colored his cheeks. But then the door slowly opened, and Maud reappeared. She was carrying the big book he had seen lying on the box beside her bed. She sat down and opened the book. It was a Bible, a family Bible, with a tooled leather cover and fancy handwriting on the first few pages. She turned them slowly and gently until she came to a photograph lodged among the pages.

"Bring the candle and come look," she said.

He removed the candle from the shelf where the crow perched. It squawked a complaint at being left in the shadows. Johnny held the candle over Maud's shoulder and peered at the photograph. It was a group picture, but it was so badly stained that it was difficult to distinguish individual people.

She pointed to a female figure and said with bittersweet sadness, "Old Maud." He strained closer with the light. She was pointing to a pretty young girl about his own age. She stood between a tall man dressed formally with a stovepipe hat, and a beautiful young Indian woman in buckskins.

"You? Old Maud?" he said incredulously. The face of the man was obliterated, but the young girl and the woman beside her looked very much alike.

"Yes. Old Maud before the fire," she said.

"Fire?" Johnny asked. Even more incredible than seeing Maud as an attractive young girl was the vague notion that he had seen the photograph before. But where, and when? And what fire?

Maud snapped the book shut, bringing him back from a deep search of his memory.

"You must prepare to leave now. It is late. I will help you wrap and tie the dog on your sled. Heavy snow is on the way. You must not make a habit of coming into the mine for any reason. It is dangerous in deep snow and during the spring thaw. In the summer when I see you in the woods, we will greet each other. We are friends now."

With those words, Johnny understood that she had his safety in mind, but also that she had lived alone for a very long time and obviously preferred it. He respected that, but was saddened to leave her alone.

Together they secured Chum on the sled, then she accompanied them to the mouth of the canyon. There, Johnny offered his hand, and she took it in both of hers.

"Thank you, Maud, for the light in the shaft and for healing Chum. My family and I are deeply grateful. You are always welcome in our home." He spoke sincerely, although he knew that she would not likely accept his invitation. She nodded her head slightly, and then turned to go. At the edge of the embankment, he looked back and saw her wave her lantern. Johnny swung his lantern in return.

All the way home, he racked his brain trying to remember where he had seen the image of that small pretty face and those big, pale eyes.

 *Nine*

In a few weeks Chum had completely healed, just as Maud said he would. Almost every day after school, Johnny and his friends romped in the deep snow with Chum to tone and strengthen his muscles. No one knew of their visit with Old Maud except Johnny's own family. His father had sworn them all to secrecy at the supper table the night that Johnny brought Chum home.

Although the family had picked up the threads of their everyday lives, during the quiet times Johnny remembered the face in the picture, and wondered whether Maud was all right up there alone in the mine. He tried to stop worrying, knowing that she had survived on her own long before he was even born.

One night, as Johnny descended the stairs after putting the little ones to bed, he clearly heard Big John say, " . . . after the tavern fire." Big John was telling yet another story to Nathan, Billy, and Mary in front of the fire, and the phrase struck a chord in Johnny's memory.

"What tavern fire, Grandfather?" he asked as he joined the others.

"Why, I was just telling the story about that big black bear that stole food from the camp cook wagon back in the old days. You've heard that story before, Son. You all have, I know. It's a wonderful story though, isn't it?"

"But you said it happened right after the tavern fire. I want to hear about that fire, Grandfather," Johnny said, struggling to make a connection between two disparate thoughts.

"Well, now, that's a very sad tale, Johnny. It happened a long time ago."

None of the others had ever before heard the story of the tavern fire, and they pressed Big John to tell it. He furrowed his brow as he strained his memory.

"Please try to remember, Grandfather," said Johnny.

"Yes, yes. Now it's coming back. My father told me the story long ago. I'll try to remember it as best I can." Big John refilled his pipe, put a match to the bowl and puffed a few times, then began.

"Well, I think it was about 1872 or '73 when the mine was running full steam. There was much more activity around here then. A lot of people lived in the valley and worked in the mine.

"A Frenchman by the name of Fournier came from up the line. He bought a little land just south of the tracks near Cobequid Crossing, and built a tavern. It was a nice little place, and the miners would stop there after work for a pint or two. A lot of the wives in the village didn't like it, though, especially after Fournier hired one of my father's younger sisters to work as a barmaid. Well, pretty soon Fournier married my aunt, the barmaid—for the life of me I can't remember her name. Anyway, they had one child, a girl, who grew up to be quite good looking. She had dark hair like her mother, and blue eyes after her father. All the young men wanted to court her when she came of age, but she was interested in only one boy, a handsome French lad who worked in the mine nights, and took lessons from the village schoolteacher whenever he could. The Fournier girl and he planned to marry, in spite of his parents' disapproval.

"One night, the boy's father became enraged after a few pints at the tavern, and warned Fournier to keep his 'half-breed daughter' away from his son. Fournier struck him, and threw him out of the tavern. Late that same night the fire bells sounded, and the village turned out to fight one of the biggest fires in the history of this valley. The tavern went up like tinder. The Fournier family perished. The bodies were found in the root cellar. There was hardly anything left. The inferno just caved in on them. It was a horrible tragedy. I was just a youngster, but I remember my father talking about it."

Johnny sat rooted to his chair. He imagined the sight of the burning tavern, and the bucket brigade that tried to put out the rising flames. Billy sat quietly stroking Chum and shaking his head. Nathan and Mary gazed sadly into the flames on the hearth.

"Where is the spot where the tavern burned?" Johnny asked.

"It's right behind the Big Rock near the Cobequid Road railroad crossing," his grandfather answered. "I believe that you children call it the 'bald spot.' Nothing has grown there all these years, not even weeds. Strange, isn't it?"

Big John studied his extinguished pipe, and then the mantle clock.

"Just look at the time," he said. He rose stiffly from his chair and bid them all good night.

One by one, the family retired for the night. Johnny lingered by the fire, waiting for it to die back enough to close the damper. His thoughts returned to Maud. As he reached up to blow out the lamp, Big John's bedroom door opened, and he came padding out carrying his old album of photographs.

"I found an old picture of my aunt who married the Frenchman Fournier, the tavern owner. I still can't remember *her* name. Would you like to see it?"

Johnny had seen his grandfather's old photographs many times before, but having just heard the story of the tavern fire, his interest was aroused and he wanted to see the photograph of the poor souls who perished.

"Sure, Grandfather," he said. "I'll turn up the lamp."

They sat at the kitchen table, and Big John spread out the album. He looked at the pictures on the left-hand page. The one he wanted to show Johnny was not among them. Peering closely over his spectacles at the page on the right, he located the photograph he wanted, and jabbed his finger at a tall, beautiful woman standing beside a bearded white man dressed in formal clothes and a stovepipe hat. Johnny pulled the lamp closer and squinted at the picture.

"That's Fournier," said Big John. "The tall woman beside him was his wife, my father's sister, Rachael . . . Rachael—that's it! That was her name!" Big John's voice seemed to fade as Johnny's eyes focused on the pretty young girl standing in front of the tall woman. She had long, silky dark hair and soft, pale eyes. It was a picture of the same young girl that Maud had shown him! *Maud before the fire!*

Johnny pointed excitedly to the young girl. "And who is this, Grandfather, this girl standing beside your Aunt Rachael?"

Big John took a closer look. "Why, that's their daughter and only child. Yes. I remember. She died in the fire, too. The year was 1891. She was just sixteen years old."

"No, Grandfather. No, no. That's Old Maud!" Johnny cried. "That's Maud!"

Big John straightened and looked into Johnny's eyes. "What are you talking about, Son? What are you saying?"

Johnny left his grandfather sitting dumbfounded. He took the stairs two at a time to Billy's room, with Chum following and barking excitedly. He pounded on the door and yelled, "Uncle Billy. It's Old Maud! The picture. It's Maud, I tell you!" Billy opened his door just as Johnny turned to his parents' bedroom door, knocking frantically. "Father, Mother, it's Maud! It's Maud!" His excitement rose until his voice cracked.

Billy spun Johnny around. "What are you saying? I don't understand."

Johnny's parents rushed out of their room. "Please, Johnny," his mother whispered. "You'll wake the children."

"Come downstairs. Please! The picture," Johnny pleaded in more hushed tones. He turned and ran downstairs, where Big John waited, perplexed.

"He saw something in the album," Big John said weakly to Mary. Johnny turned up the lamp so high that the flame blackened the glass chimney.

"Look. Here," he said, trying to calm himself. "This is a photograph of Old Maud before the fire!" He repeated Maud's own words. But he could tell by his family's expressions that they did-n't understand his babbling, although to him it was crystal clear. He began to explain as calmly as he could.

"The night I brought Chum home from Maud's cabin, she showed me her family Bible. In it was a duplicate of this same photograph of her with her mother and father. I couldn't make out her father's face because the picture was so badly damaged. But his clothes are identical. The tall woman was in the picture, too. This woman is Maud's mother, Grandfather's *Aunt Rachael!*"

He continued breathlessly. "Maud showed me this young girl in an identical photograph and said, 'Old Maud before the fire.' That's all she said. I tell you, it's Maud. She didn't die in the fire. She escaped with her family Bible. I don't know how she did it, but she did. She must have found her way to a relative in the next valley, because after the mine closed, she said that this 'kins-man' helped her build her cabin in the canyon. She's been up there in the mine alone all these years," Johnny wailed. "And the rea-son she doesn't come down and live in the village is because her face and head were burned so badly. That's how she lost her eye," he moaned, his brain working overtime to fill in the blanks. "She says she frightens the children," he explained bitterly, the cruel stories once more making him cringe.

There was a long silence while each of them considered the significance of this astonishing discovery.

"Could this be true?" Nathan asked. They looked again at the photograph, then at Big John.

Big John spoke quietly, offering the best explanation he could.

"They couldn't identify the remains. There was so little left. She was sixteen when it happened. The authorities could never prove how the fire started. The villagers believed that it was her lover's father who was responsible. Soon after, he took his family and moved away. No one knew where. Some say her sweetheart died of consumption, others of a broken heart. I wish I could re-member their name," he mused. "But that is not important now. If, in fact, Maud *did* escape the fire, we must do something right away. We must acknowledge her as our kin and—"

Johnny interrupted, "But she *did* escape, Grandfather. She has her family Bible to prove it. She knows my name, where we live, and things about our family." Each of them looked incredulously at one another.

"I believe it," said Billy with conviction. "I believe she came back to be near the only family she has left. This valley is her home as much as it is ours. She grew up here just like we all did. Why, Maud would be your first cousin, Father, and almost seventy years old," he calculated. "A very old lady, living alone and unprotected."

Big John's eyes grew dark with sadness and concern. "I'm convinced this is all true, but what shall we do now?"

"Nothing can be done tonight, nor tomorrow, for that matter," said Nathan helplessly. "There's no way we can get through to her now. We'll have to wait until the weather breaks. As soon as it's safe, we'll go to the mine and find her," he announced, his voice growing stronger. "We'll take Johnny along as our guide and spokesman. We'll persuade her to come live with us. As a blood member of our family, she'll take her place at our table. She'll be comfortable here on the Lightfoot farm." Nathan turned to Mary, who smiled proudly up at him with her eyes full of tears.

The discussion of Maud continued far into the night. Johnny told them how he admired her independence and, most of all, her kindness and unselfishness in the face of the hardship, rejection, and scorn she had suffered most of her life.

After everyone had gone back to bed, Johnny wondered what it would be like to have Maud live on their farm. They would be famous—or infamous, depending upon their neighbors' points of view when they discovered the truth about Maud. The thought was definitely exciting, and also amusing. How the tongues would wag at Milligan's Store! On the other hand, when he considered Maud's long life as a hermit, he doubted that she would agree to share their home. Yet she must have wanted the Lightfoot family to know who she was, how she had kept in touch but kept her distance, and that she cared about them.

 ## Ten

Johnny cleaned the soot from the lamp chimney and took the sparkling lamp upstairs to his room. He said his prayers and kissed Chum's head before climbing into bed. He felt happy with his discovery, and excited about the prospect of helping to provide for Maud as one of the family. He thought that a nice cabin might be built for her on their land if she refused to live in their house. The Lightfoot family would certainly see to it that she had proper quarters and good food wherever she chose to live. In the morning he would share these thoughts and ideas with his parents in the morning.

But Johnny slept very little that night. Snatches of dreams and visions of Maud's flight from her parents' burning home tugged him back to wakefulness.

Months had passed since he last saw Maud in the mine. There were questions he wanted to ask her, and regretted not having had the courage to ask them when he had the chance. What a nitwit he was not to have recognized her photograph right away. If only he had known then that Maud was his grandfather's cousin. The discovery would have removed every trace of fear from his heart, and replaced it with love and understanding. He would have thrown his arms around Maud as easily and comfortably as he did any of his other relatives. It would have made such a difference to her. How it must have hurt her to see him recoil from the sight of her face! Because it had taken him so long to put the pieces together, she had spent the better part of another winter alone in the mine, with no word from her family. He groaned aloud with remorse and couldn't get back to sleep.

Finally, he heard his father making a fire in the woodstove down in the kitchen. Johnny got out of bed and looked out the window. A new light snow was falling, and the hazy moon, now low over the trees, reflected its light off a million tiny, shimmering snow crystals floating down from the sky. It was still dark at 4:00 a.m. Johnny usually rose at five o'clock, when the kitchen was warmed, a luxury he still enjoyed with his brother and little sisters. But this morning he wanted to share the extra hour with his father. Chum rose and stretched at the foot of the bed, yawned and shook himself, then followed Johnny down to the kitchen.

"Morning, Son. What are you doing up so early?"

"I couldn't sleep. I've been thinking about Maud. Don't you think we should let her know right away that we know who she is?"

"The weather won't break until at least the end of March, Johnny. We can't go up there now. There's more than three feet of snow on the ground."

"If we don't let her know, she'll think we don't care. It's almost March. It's nearly four months since I last saw her. What if she's sick? What if she's . . . ?" Johnny couldn't bring himself to say the word. "What about snowshoes? Three feet of snow never stopped us from hunting. The three of us can go—you, me, and Uncle Billy."

"We don't know the mine like we know the woods, Johnny. There are pitfalls in the mine. There are no reliable landmarks or trees to mark a trail. It's just too dangerous."

Nathan shook his head and held his hands above the stove to warm them. As though something suddenly crossed his mind, he turned a hard glance at his son. "You're not thinking . . . ."

Johnny tried to keep the disappointment from his voice. "No, Father. I give you my solemn word."

Billy watched Johnny all morning while they did their chores. He knew that his nephew was trying to think of a way to contact Maud. He could almost see the wheels turning in Johnny's head. Later that day, at the woodpile down by the barn, Billy stopped splitting wood long enough to make a silly suggestion.

"Now, if Chum were a Saint Bernard, we could tie a message on a collar around his neck and send him into the mine to find Maud."

Johnny frowned. He would never send Chum on such a dangerous mission, Saint Bernard or not.

"The snow is too deep. Chum would try, but he'd never make it. He'd tire himself out and get stranded up there. He wouldn't last an hour in this cold."

"You're right, Johnny. *That* is not a good idea."

"But I've been thinking," Johnny said. "What if we go ask Mr. Norris, the government man, to put a note out in his secret tree on Cobequid Road? You know, the one with the knothole where he sets out stuff for Maud. We could ask him to hang a red bandanna on the tree just to make sure she knew there was something in there for her."

Billy glanced at Johnny out of the corner of his eye. His ax came down on a piece of firewood set vertically on the chopping block, sending the two halves flying in opposite directions.

"Now that's a brilliant idea. Why didn't I think of that? Except, I don't know how she'd manage to get down to Cobequid Road, or why she would want to in this weather." Billy stood another log on the chopping block.

"Oh, Maud wouldn't have any trouble in the deep snow," Johnny said confidently. "Maybe she'll run out of food and tobacco. She smokes a pipe, you know," Johnny said with the pride of knowing such things about Maud.

Just before sundown the next day, they saddled up Ruby and rode double to Mr. Norris's little house at the end of Mine Hill. In Johnny's pocket was the sealed note for Maud. He had read it to his family, inquiring before sealing it if they wanted to add anything. He wrote sincerely of his family's joy at discovering who she was from an identical photograph in Big John's possession, and their wish to have her come live with them on the Lightfoot farm. He borrowed a red bandanna from his grandfather for Mr. Norris to hang on the tree on Cobequid Road.

Johnny and Billy rode in silence, enjoying the cold, crisp twilight and the trees silhouetted against the soft layers of copper and blue-green sky. The snow flew in clumps from under the mare's hooves as she trotted along contentedly in the earlier tracks of other horses. She snorted now and then as though charmed by the frosty white plumes of her own warm breath. A late-season loon, its underwings illuminated by the last rays of the setting sun, flew overhead on the way to a winter roost at the end of Loon Lake, to the east.

Herb Norris came to the door with a steaming cup in his hand. He seemed surprised yet pleased to see them. They declined his offer of coffee and got right down to business.

Johnny explained what he wanted Mr. Norris to do, without telling him the contents of the note. The family had agreed on that. Mr. Norris, of course, was curious about their reasons for contacting Old Maud, but he agreed to put the note in the tree and hang the bandanna to attract her attention. After all, he knew that the Lightfoot family was part Micmac, and he suspected that Old Maud was, too. They probably wanted some roots and herbs, or maybe some kind of special potion that only she could provide. Anyway, he felt that it was really none of his business. The Lightfoots had never given him any trouble, and he saw no reason to refuse their request.

"To tell you the truth, though," said Mr. Norris, "I don't think Old Maud's been around since before Christmas. I remember because I put some dried cod and salt mackerel in the tree a couple days before Christmas, and they were gone the next morning." He saw no need to mention her gift to him: the little gold nugget, carefully wrapped in a scrap of butcher paper on which was written "Merry Christmas," and placed in a tobacco tin in the knothole. He had been touched. "But she didn't take the tobacco I left on Christmas Day, so I took it out of the hole. Maybe I'll just put some fresh tobacco in with your note. How's that?"

"That would be fine," said Billy. "If you could just let us know if and when the note is picked up, we'd be much obliged."

"I can certainly do that," said Mr. Norris.

They left him with the note and bandanna, and rode home in the dark, arriving just as Johnny's mother was putting supper on the table.

Three weeks passed without a word from Mr. Norris. Johnny was anxious and disappointed. When Billy had seen Herb several times at Milligan's Store, he had just shaken his head and said, "Nothing yet."

Time seemed to drag while Johnny waited for the weather to break. He and his friends searched the skies for robins and migrating waterfowl—harbingers of an early spring. He prevailed upon Big John to walk with him and Chum on the thick ice of Loon Lake to study the tracks of mink, muskrat, and beaver. On their second time out, the ice resounded with a powerful and frightening shudder. Johnny, thinking the ice was giving way, threw himself down, spread eagled, the way he had been taught. Big John laughed and helped him to his feet.

"That was the sign you've been waiting for, Son. The snow is melting and the lake water is rising. Spring is right under our feet."

Later that day, Herb Norris tapped on their kitchen door just as the family was sitting down to supper.

"Why, Mr. Norris," said Mary Lightfoot, loud enough for everyone to hear. "How nice to see you, and just in time for supper."

Herb pulled off his wool cap, causing static electricity to lift the thin hair straight up from his bald spot. He handed the cap to Mary while the little ones tried to stifle giggles with their palms pressed hard against their mouths. Almost as an afterthought, he took a small tobacco tin sealed with candle wax from his pocket and handed it to Mary. Then he rushed to the table and pulled up an extra chair.

"Pull up a chair and have some dinner," Big John said, with a wink at Nathan.

Mary handed the tin to Big John, who passed it to Johnny. "Where's the red bandanna?" Big John asked.

"The red bandanna?" repeated Herb, frowning at the ceiling and ceasing to chew as though unable to think and chew at the same time. "Uh, . . . it wasn't there. Old Maud must have taken it with her."

Johnny immediately excused himself from the table and rushed to his room. He hastily opened the tin and unfolded a scrap of paper upon which were written these words:

"Please do not worry. I am well. We will talk soon." It was signed, "Maud Fournier."

Eleven

Spring came early to the region, and it was exceptionally wet. The Lightfoot family received shipments of vegetable and flower seeds, onion sets, and new apple tree saplings almost daily. Portions of Loon Lake were open, and loons were seen diving for minnows, while Canada geese and mallards foraged for tender green shoots in the shallows. Quacking loudly to one another, the ducks stabbed the frigid water with their bills, their tail feathers bobbing skyward.

Maud had been sighted fishing in the swollen creek several miles south of the village—news that somewhat relieved Johnny's anxiety. On the other hand, at Milligan's Store, he heard the men talking about the mudslides in the hills just a mile west of the mine—another source of concern.

At supper that evening, Johnny was quiet and pushed the food around on his plate. Maud had not contacted the family since her message had come three weeks before. The family discussed it, and Big John felt that they should wait for Maud to tell them when to come to her.

"She knows our concerns for her welfare," he reminded Johnny. "She said we would talk 'soon,' so we have to be patient.

Besides, the weather is bad, and the conditions in the mine are still dangerous. We'll just have to wait."

Nathan agreed.

"If only the rain would stop," Johnny complained.

The clouds finally broke toward the end of the following week. When the woods dried out a little, Billy suggested that they all go mushroom hunting. The younger children squealed with excitement and ran around finding baskets and rubber boots to wear into the soggy forest.

Johnny waited until almost everyone had left the house. Then he went to his room, lay on his bed, and tried to figure out what to do about Maud.

There was a tap on his door. It was Billy.

"Aren't you coming with us?"

"I'm sorry, Uncle Billy. I don't have the heart for it. I think I'll just stay here."

"But we've all been cooped up in this house for weeks. I thought you especially would welcome a chance to go into the woods. Are you all right?"

"Actually," Johnny replied, "I thought I'd go over to a friend's house for a while."

"Oh, that's a good idea. For a minute there I thought you were still worried about Maud. You should know by now that she's very capable of taking care of herself. We'll hear from her. You'll see." He turned to join the others for the mushroom hunt.

"To tell you the truth, I was thinking of going to see Mr. Norris to ask him to check the tree again. Maybe there's another message," Johnny admitted.

Billy came back and sat down beside Johnny. He put an arm around his shoulders.

"Listen to me, Johnny. We're all worried about Maud, especially your grandfather. He wants to put an end to her loneliness, and somehow make up for the misery she's suffered all these years. But I want you to think about this: Maud has been on her own for a very long time. A capable person like that has learned better than any of us how to survive in the wild. She's as familiar with the mine as we are with our farm. It's her home, and she's come to terms with it. She has instincts as keen as any animal living in the wilderness. True, she's old, but she's hardy. She's a keen hunter and smart, too. She knows what wild plants, roots, and nuts make good food, what herbs to use for medicine, and all those good things that come from the earth. You and Chum know that better than anybody. And she has pride, Micmac pride. We Lightfoots know what that means, don't we?"

Johnny nodded yes.

Billy went on. "Those superstitious people in the village say she does witchcraft, but that's because they don't understand her circumstances the way we do now. It's a mystery to them how she survives on her own. They believe she must have special powers that they're afraid she'll use against them. They'll feel differently when they find out who she really is. Right now they see only what they want to see—a mysterious, ugly old lady who appeared from seemingly nowhere."

"But she's not ugly," Johnny protested. "Her face is scarred, but there's something about her way, her . . ." He struggled to find the right words.

"I know what you mean, Johnny. Her kindness and goodness shine through. You can see beyond the scars."

"Yes, that's exactly it."

"Well, we're very lucky to have found Maud. She'll be one of us, and she'll make our home even happier."

Johnny suddenly felt better. He smiled broadly at his uncle, jumped up from the bed, and headed for the stairs. Then he stuck his head back into the open doorway and called out, "Well, come on. We have to catch up!"

By the time they reached the edge of the woods, the others were nowhere in sight.

Johnny and Billy—with Chum close on their heels—headed in the direction of the lake, then skirted to the west end to a spot where they had seen a good crop of wild mushrooms the year before. They had stopped talking, busy with mushroom picking, when they saw a clearing that sloped to a little sandy beach at the water's edge. Chum suddenly stopped. With an uplifted nose that formed a perfect line along his back to his rigid tail, he pointed straight ahead. Johnny and Billy stopped in their tracks and fell to their knees.

Billy whispered to Johnny, "There's something in the clearing. I think we're downwind. Stay close to the ground. I'll go up to see what it is."

He crept silently on all fours to where Chum was pointing. He pushed the dog's body down to a crouching position, circled the dog's muzzle with one hand to keep him quiet, and peered through the brush at the edge of the clearing. As Johnny watched, he saw Billy relax, then beckon him to follow quietly on his hands and knees.

About twenty feet from shore, standing in water up to its knees, was a great bull moose with a full rack. Billy put a hand on Johnny's arm and a finger to his pursed lips, signaling him to keep down behind a low bush and stay quiet.

Johnny had never before seen a moose this close. The animal was bigger than a horse and stood much taller at the hump above the shoulder. Its brown-gray coat was shaggy and beginning to shed. As close as Billy could estimate, the velvety antlers on its massive head measured a good six feet across. The animal stood ready to drink, its broad muzzle and pendulous beard poised just above the surface of the water.

They watched awestruck until Johnny caught a glimpse of red across the lake—a movement on the opposite shore near the tree line. He tugged his uncle's sleeve and pointed in that direction. They squinted in the sunlight until they perceived the figure of a person moving slowly along the rocky ledge.

"It's Maud!" Johnny yelled, jumping up from behind the bushes. The moose raised its magnificent head, dripping water from its grizzled beard. It looked directly into Johnny's eyes for a split second, then, with a mighty splash, it lunged from the water and ran crashing into the woods.

Johnny dashed into the clearing and down to the little beach, wildly waving his arms and jumping up and down. He cupped his hands around his mouth and called out at the top of his lungs.

"Maud, Maud! Over here, Maud! It's me, Johnny! Hello, Maud!"

Chum emerged from the woods, lifted his nose, and smelled the air. He began barking excitedly, running up and down the embankment. He splashed into the water and started swimming out, until he realized that Johnny was still on dry land. He returned to the beach, whining and barking in the direction of the opposite shore.

Their voices carried over the water. Maud stopped and looked up, raised a hand to shade her eyes, and pulled the red bandanna from her head. She waved it slowly aloft in recognition. Then she turned, retied the bandanna, and continued on her way.

Johnny was elated to see Maud, but he was somewhat disappointed, too. Had his family's canoes been on the lake for the season, he could easily have paddled to the other shore in minutes.

He walked back to where Billy was waiting for him.

"That was Maud," he said, embarrassed at having scared off the moose. "It looked like she was waving Grandfather's bandanna."

"I believe you're right. And I think it means something special," said Billy.

"You do? What do you think it means?" asked Johnny.

"I think it means that Cousin Maud is ready to powwow with the Lightfoot family."

His words didn't register for a second or two. Billy waited, smiling, watching the pieces go together in Johnny's head, and his eyes grow wider.

Johnny's spirits soared anew. A broad smile lifted his face. "You're right! That's exactly what it means." He playfully punched his uncle's shoulder. "It couldn't mean anything else. Yaa-hoo!" he shouted. "Let's go home and tell Grandfather!"

Herb Norris locked the gate behind him. The chain-link fence was seven feet high and the gate just wide enough to allow his pickup truck to pass through. The rivulets of water running down Mine Hill had eroded some of the dirt and gravel at the base of the concrete footings, and he shook the uprights to test their strength. He was worried, too, about the mudslides, which he had already reported to the government officials.

Today his inspection would take him farther up into the mine to check on any cave-in activity that might have occurred over the last few days of heavy downpours. The rain had stopped temporarily, but the day was dark and gloomy. He drove the pickup slowly and carefully up Mine Hill, keeping well away from the unstable shoulders of the steep road. At the top of the hill he took a heavy, five-foot steel bar from the truck bed and hoisted it over his shoulder.

When he reached the clearing, he followed the old, rusty ore-car tracks to a small rise, where he saw, in the distance, several piles of ore dumped from excavations dug years ago. He sighed heavily, wishing he didn't have to do what was required by the Department of Mines, and stepped away from the tracks. As he walked toward the old sinkhole, he repeatedly thrust the heavy iron bar into the ground ahead of him.

He continued this procedure until, about forty yards from the tracks, he came upon a small depression in the gravelly surface. He stopped. Stepping about five feet back from the edge of the depression, he aimed the bar at its center. When he withdrew it, the muddy gravel began to move. Herb watched like a man charmed by a deadly snake as a dark, slowly widening hole appeared in the middle of the depression. Then, terrified, he let the steel bar fall from his hand. The center of the depression suddenly gave way with a sickening thud as a six-foot-wide hole yawned open. Herb turned quickly to run back to the tracks, but tripped over the steel bar lying on the ground behind him. On all fours, he scrambled away in panic.

When he was able to regain his footing, he ran as fast as he could back to the tracks. He could hear the earth and timbers collapsing upon themselves, roaring and trembling behind him as they plunged into a deep underground shaft. Like a living thing, the tunnel continued to swallow the earth along its length to within a few yards of the tracks. Then it stopped. Horror-stricken, Herb ran between the rails as though chased by a demon, until he finally reached the clearing where his truck was parked. He quickly climbed behind the wheel and held his breath. All was silent. He was too frightened to go back down the tracks to inspect what had just happened.

When the Lightfoot family returned home with baskets brimming with various kinds of mushrooms, they found Herb Norris sitting on the bench by the kitchen door. At his feet was a burlap sack whose contents poked out at peculiar angles. He was obviously agitated about having to wait. He looked at his watch and scowled as the family approached the house.

Mary and the children said their hello's anyway and went into the house to sort the bounty.

"Well, Herb, to what do we owe this visit?" Big John asked.

"It's late," Herb complained. "I can't stay for supper tonight, Big John." He removed his wool cap and wiped his brow with a big blue checkered handkerchief. "I've been up in the mine. Conditions are terrible up there." He related his experience of the day before.

"I made some signs to post, hoping to keep the villagers out. Problem is, I don't know all the paths they've been using. The whole mine is like a mountain of Swiss cheese. This is no joke. I've never seen the water so high in the old sinkhole. When I tested the ground near the ore-car tracks, a whole section gave way. I thought I was a goner, let me tell you. I'm going to post these signs at Milligan's Store, on the telegraph poles in the village, and the rest around the perimeter of the mine." He poked the burlap sack with his foot. "Oh, by the way, give this to Johnny," he said, pulling a small package from his jacket pocket. "I found it in the tree on the way down here. And here's the bandanna. This tobacco tin was sealed with candle wax and wrapped in the bandanna. It's none of my business, of course, but what's going on between Old Maud and the Lightfoots? Need a potion—a spell maybe?" Herb chuckled.

"Sorry, Herb. Can't discuss it right now. If you're going to nail up those signs before dark, you'd better get started," Big John advised as he opened the kitchen door to go inside. "See you soon. Let us know if there are any more cave-ins."

Inside, Big John said to Mary, "When Johnny comes home, tell him there's word from Maud." Then he went to his room to open the tin.

Big John broke the seal with trembling fingers and withdrew the piece of yellow-brown paper. It smelled of sweet tobacco.

"Cousin. The mine is very dangerous now. You must not come by the old path. You and Johnny meet me after sunup on the Sabbath at the clearing above Mine Hill. Do not venture farther without me. Maud Fournier."

Big John folded the paper and replaced it in the tin. His heart pounded with anticipation of seeing Maud after so many years.

Thinking about his distant glimpses of her in the woods years ago was painful for him now. If only he had known.

Big John lay back on his pillow and tried to remember the old times, those special times in the valley when many Micmac families came together to council from as far away as Cape Breton Island, Newfoundland, New Brunswick, and Maine. He had been just a child, occupied with things of interest only to small boys of his tribe—horses, hunting, fishing, and camping in the woods. He had no memory of events or people outside his immediate family and closest playmates. Try as he might, he could not personally recall Maud as a young girl. He had no recollection of the tavern, and only a vague memory of the fire that claimed the lives of Maud's parents. He remembered only his father's telling of the tale and the sorrow that the event had brought to his father in the telling. In fact, the images described were so vivid in his mind that sometimes Big John thought he had personally witnessed the tragedy. He hoped he could somehow make it up to Maud, not for the loss of her parents, or for the trials she must have suffered all alone—he could never do that—but in the security and comfort he could provide for the rest of her life on the Lightfoot farm. He would spare nothing to make her happy.

A light tap on his door roused him from his daydreams.

"Come in, Johnny. I've been waiting for you."

Johnny stuck his head in the doorway. His face beamed. "Mother told me that Maud sent word," he said excitedly. "Uncle Billy and I saw her across the lake just this morning. She waved your bandanna at us. Uncle Billy said it was a signal, and he was right."

Big John held out the tin wrapped in the bandanna. "Herb brought it here about an hour ago. She must have put it in the tree after you saw her," he said, reflecting on how Maud so ably navigated the woods.

Johnny read the note while Big John watched the excitement grow in his eyes.

"Oh, Grandfather. Just two more days until Sunday! Let's hope for the good weather to hold."

Johnny began pacing the room. Then he stopped, suddenly reminded of the details of the note.

"But she wants only you and me to come. Father and Uncle Billy will be disappointed." He paused. "And then there's the gate. If we can't take my usual path, we'll have to convince Mr. Norris to let us through the gate."

"Yes," said Big John. "That's the most difficult part, especially because of what's just happened in the mine." He told Johnny about the cave-ins, and Herb's posting of the warning signs all over the valley.

"We might have to take Herb into our confidence to get us through that gate," said Big John. "We'd better talk this over with your father and Billy."

Twelve

Meanwhile, on the south side of the village of Beaver Creek, Luke Graywolf and his best friend, Charlie Tatum, were again late for school. Luke was twelve, a year older than Charlie, wise for his age and inclined to be a little bossy. The boys were exact opposites in looks, character, and personality. Luke's long, shiny hair and eyes were almost black, and his skin olive, whereas Charlie's carrot top was cut short in a haphazard fashion. His eyes were emerald green, and his pinkish skin was covered with freckles. Luke was tall for his age, and thin. Charlie was inches shorter and on the chubby side.

Luke's mother had died when he was two years old. His older and only sister, Esther, was pressed into housekeeping services for their father and four other brothers, who worked at Graywolf's lumber camp. Although Luke was the youngest and still required supervision, Esther had absolutely no interest in his education, where he went, or what he did. One day Luke's teacher visited Esther and reported that Luke often played hooky from school. Seated at the other end of her kitchen table and wearing a bored expression, Esther listened to Miss Wilson's complaints and made no effort to comply with her recommendations.

The two boys were always together, except on rare occasions when they were forced to do their separate family chores or when Silky Ann Sanders caught up with them on the way to school. Silky annoyed Charlie because, when she was around, Luke acted funny and never listened to anything Charlie had to say. Besides, she was a girl, and Charlie felt she had no business horning in on his and Luke's discussions.

Charlie was the only boy in a family of six children. Luke seemed to take the place of the brother he never had, and he felt as close to Luke as any brother would. He wished that he were Micmac, like Luke. He always followed a few steps behind Luke, who was a leader, a hunter, an explorer. His desk was behind Luke's at school, where their classroom consisted of three grades to one teacher. Neither boy was a star pupil, although Charlie liked to read when Luke wasn't around.

On the days when Luke decided to go to school, he'd stop at Charlie's house on the way. They were often late for the second bell because they'd find interesting things to see or do along the way. They never tired of skipping stones across the surface of Bottomless Pond, where they walked along the muddy edge among the bulrushes, trying to catch frogs as they leaped into the water. They'd chuckle as they watched Ralph Larson's son Wally's little bantam rooster chase his hens all over the yard. And how could they not follow a mangy cat carrying her litter of kittens to a new location, or watch a turtle cry real tears as she laid her eggs in a sandy hole?

Miss Wilson sent the boys to the principal's office so many times that eventually he gave up and sent the boys back to class with a note suggesting that Miss Wilson consider the boys "unusually talented students to be dealt with on a specialized basis." Relieved from her strict disciplinary role and encouraged to utilize her creative skills, Miss Wilson asked Luke and Charlie to give an accounting of what they saw or did on the way to school on a given day. Interesting discussions with their classmates resulted, and the students became so excited and enthusiastic that Miss Wilson feared all of them might go off on their own adventures. She needn't have worried; none of her other pupils had Luke's imagination and adventurous spirit or enjoyed such freedom from strict parental authority. Luke thrived on the attention, and his attendance at school actually improved— somewhat.

Silky Ann was one of Miss Wilson's best students, and she enjoyed competing with Luke in the classroom. She was the tallest pupil in her sixth-grade class; even taller than Luke by half a head. She was Micmac on her mother's side and had her father's Irish temperament. She wore a clean dress to school every day, and sometimes her brown hair was tied up in a bow of matching color. Although Silky seemed to resent Luke's "undeserved" popularity, she liked having him in class and tried to impress him with her superior knowledge and intelligence. Unlike Silky, Luke rarely did any homework, so he was not surprised or impressed when Silky knew the answers to all Miss Wilson's questions regarding the day's lessons.

Luke thought Silky *was* interesting, as girls go. He had seen her several times on the way to church with her parents. She always wore a pretty dress and her hair flowed free like blowing wheat in a field. *She was certainly well named*, he thought. Meanwhile, Silky felt embarrassed and sad for Luke when he struggled to solve an arithmetic problem at the blackboard. Some of the students whispered about his mistakes and giggled when his back was turned.

One day she offered to help him with his arithmetic homework after school if he would let her go fishing with him sometime. He agreed reluctantly, and they sat at the picnic table in the school yard until Luke better understood fractions. Luke remarked casually that he might be passing her house on the way to Bottomless Pond the following Saturday morning.

Silky's family lived up the hill from Dawe's Road, at the end of Bottomless Pond. Luke passed their house many times on the way eel fishing. On Saturday morning, from her window, Silky watched the road with anticipation, and finally saw Luke coming up the hill. He saw her at the window, but continued past her house without stopping. She'd fully expected him to knock at the door, and maybe say hello to her parents. *He has a lot to learn about girls*, she thought. She quickly gathered her fishing gear—a tin of worms, a few safety pins, and a strong line tied to the end of a stout stick—and angrily followed Luke, at a discreet distance, to the pond.

Ignoring Silky completely, Luke took up a position at one end of the embankment, baited his hook, and threw in his line. Silky waited until he was settled and took her place about fifteen feet from him. She squeezed her eyes shut and impaled a worm on the sharp shaft of a big safety pin, tied a small stone to the end of the line, and cast it beyond where Luke's had entered the water.

He glanced over at Silky, who had been watching him, and turned quickly away.

"You ain't never gonna catch an eel with a safety pin. Not strong enough," Luke advised.

"That's what you think," Silky snapped. I bet I've caught more eels with safety pins than you with that big old hook."

"I've got another one you can borrow if you want." Luke held out a thin aspirin tin in the palm of his hand.

"No, thank you. I'll do just fine with my pin. You'll see."

The words were no sooner out when Silky felt a tug on her line. She hesitated a second to make sure it was a real bite. When the next nibble came, Silky jerked the pole straight up with both hands. A three-foot eel broke the surface, struggling against the safety pin securely embedded in its upper jaw. Running backward up the embankment, Silky gave the pole another strong jolt. The wriggling eel landed with a thud on the rocks behind her.

Luke ran to help her control the wildly flailing fish before it could escape.

"Back off, Luke!" she shouted. "He's mine!"

Still holding the pole attached to the fighting fish, Silky scrambled on all fours farther up the bank after her catch. The eel lunged and squirmed and tried to get back to the water, but it was tiring and gasping for oxygen. When the opportunity presented itself, she stomped her foot on the eel's slimy head and held it there as the fish wrapped its body around her ankle. She stifled a scream, determined to show Luke she wasn't one bit squeamish.

When the eel finally stopped struggling, Silky unwound its twitching body from her ankle and held it up for Luke to see.

"Damn! That was somethin'. Where'd you learn to fish eels with a safety pin?"

Silky was relieved that the ordeal was over. Forgetting her anger, she laughed and pointed to the eel's underbelly. The rusty point of another safety pin protruded from the fish's gut. "He must be the one that got away," she said.

"Well, I'll be . . . ," said Luke, amazed.

He removed the pin from the fish's mouth and tied the eel to Silky's pole. Chatting and laughing together as they climbed the embankment, they made plans to go fishing the next weekend if the weather held.

The next day at school Charlie, watched as Luke and Silky exchanged friendlier-than-ever glances—until Silky caught him staring and stuck her tongue out at him. When school let out, Charlie and Luke started for home together. Charlie sulked and didn't have much to say until, as though unable to hold it in any longer, he suddenly stopped in his tracks and blurted, "Is Silky your best friend now, Luke? Just because she caught a stupid old eel with a stupid safety pin, is she gonna be your girlfriend, for Pete's sake?"

"No, she ain't gonna be my girlfriend." Luke smiled at the idea. "But you gotta give her credit, Charlie. She ain't like most girls, all giggly and foolish-actin'. She ain't afraid of bugs, or baiting a hook, or walkin' home alone after dark. She went and caught *the biggest eel of the season* and fought it to the death. And, what about that big spider she brought to school a while back? Remember that?"

Charlie kicked a stone with the toe of his boot. He remembered that day, all right. He and Luke had found a perfectly preserved hornets' nest that they had brought to school to show their classmates. Theirs was the best exhibit of the day, until Silky raised her hand to ask Miss Wilson if she could show what *she* had brought. With that sweet smile of hers, Silky took a glass jar from her desk. With the label still intact, the contents were hidden. She unscrewed the cap and placed it on the desk, then upended the jar and shook out a huge and most disgusting spider of unknown species. The creature had black hairy legs and a shiny bulbous body. Most fascinating were its eight oddly blue eyes.

All the girls and a few boys gasped and shrank back against the walls as the spider uncurled itself and started crawling along the top of Silky's desk. Miss Wilson seemed spellbound, but finally found her voice.

"Thank you, Silky Ann. We've seen quite enough. You may put the spider back in the jar now."

Silky quickly placed the mouth of the jar over the spider. It grasped the small twig inside the jar and disappeared behind the label. Silky clapped the lid back on, turned to Luke, and smiled again. *Showoff*, thought Charlie. He was equally disgusted later, when Luke rushed off to find Silky after class to ask where she had found such an admirable arachnid.

The following Saturday morning, Silky, Luke, and Charlie set out for Bottomless Pond to fish for eels. Despite himself, Charlie had been impressed with Luke's account of Silky's catch the week before. She might not be half bad as girls go, as long as she understood that he and Luke wouldn't always tolerate the presence of a girl. They had almost reached their destination on the other side of the tracks near Cobequid Road, when Graywolf and Esther overtook them in the pickup. Graywolf slammed on the brakes and stopped in front of them on the roadside.

"Just where do you think you're goin'?" he demanded of Luke, who had left the house before his father was awake.

"I'm goin'. . . we're goin' . . ."

"You're goin' with Esther and me to pick up supplies, that's where you're goin'. Now, get in back. You, too, Charlie."

Graywolf glanced at Silky. "And who are you? Does your mother know where you are?"

Silky had heard of Luke's gruff father, and she wasn't about to let Tom Graywolf intimidate her. "My mother *always* knows where *I* am," she said defiantly. She looked up at Luke in the back of the truck. "Are you going fishing with me or not?"

"No, he ain't goin' fishin' with you," Graywolf answered for Luke, who seemed ashamed of his father's angry tone. "And don't you sass me, missy. Now, you go on home where you belong."

Graywolf stepped on the gas and sped off toward Milligan's store. From the back of the truck, Charlie waved gaily at Silky standing alone in the middle of the road, sticking out her tongue at all of them.

After dropping off Charlie at home, Graywolf, Esther, and Luke pulled up in front of Mr. Milligan's store at the same time that Herb Norris arrived with his signs. Inside, Max Fox and Old Man Callahan were talking with Mrs. Milligan. Herb posted the warning signs, one in the store window and another beside the post office wicket. Max strode over to the post office section to read Herb's hand-lettered notice. "DANGER," it read in bright red letters. "NEW CAVE-INS AT THE MINE. KEEP OUT."

Max turned to Herb. "What's goin' on up there?"

"I'm telling you, Max. If the folks in Beaver Creek don't heed this warning, I'm afraid there'll be tragic circumstances. I've been testing the ground near the ore-car tracks. About a hundred-foot section of tunnel caved in on itself there and nearly swallowed me up! I barely got back to the tracks in time. It was the most godaw-ful thing I've ever seen or heard in my life. The ground shook like a huge underground monster struggling to free itself.

"The sinkhole is full to overflowing. The water pressure's bound to cause seepage into the shafts and tunnels. Think about it—the timbers are old and rotten. They can't hold back those wet walls for long. God knows how many miles of shaft are filling with water after all that rain. There'll be new holes opening up, exposing shafts and tunnels nobody's seen since the mine closed.

"Warn your neighbors, Cal," Herb said, turning to Mr. Callahan. "The young fellas around here think that pulling the wool over old Herb's eyes is a joke. But this is serious business. We don't want to see anybody buried alive up there."

Herb picked up his burlap sack of signs and started for the door. "That goes for you, too, young fella," he said, turning to glare at Luke Graywolf.

Luke was grateful that Mr. Norris didn't spill the beans about his forays into the mine. Last summer, Herb had caught Luke climbing down the outcropping near Larson's farm as he was leaving one of the old mine tunnels.

"You heard what the man said," Tom Graywolf growled at Luke. "You stay outta that mine, or I'll skin your hide."

Luke mocked his father's words under his breath. *Don't do this*, and *don't do that, or I'll skin your hide* were Tom Graywolf's standard—and empty—warning. It was seldom that his father paid him any real attention or followed through on those threats. Because Tom Graywolf rarely knew what Luke was up to on a day-to-day basis anyway, there were no questions asked as long as Luke appeared for supper by the time his father and brothers came home from the lumber camp. Luke's troubles were never the result of mischief for its own sake. It was just that his curiosity and his need to explore always got the better of him, and the mine provided outstanding opportunities to exercise his imagination.

Early the next morning, Luke rose before anyone else. It was still dark when he crossed the yard to the chicken coop. He opened the wire gate and closed it quietly behind him. As he opened the coop door, some of the chickens, still on the roost, cackled and threatened to make a fuss. Luke reached up and felt around over the door jamb for a loose shingle. From behind it he removed a small cotton marble bag with a drawstring top. After carefully replacing the shingle, he stepped backward out the door and closed it.

When he returned to the house, Esther was slinging great gobs of steaming porridge into seven bowls on the table. Her hair was in curler rags, and he wondered why she bothered. His sister was one of the plainest and most uninteresting people he knew, and her poker-straight hair was the least of it.

"Where you been, Luke? You just comin' in from roamin' all night?" she asked without looking at her brother.

"No, I ain't been roamin'. But I ain't been sleepin' neither. Your snorin' woke up the chickens, and I been calmin' 'em down."

"Very funny. Now sit down and eat," Esther replied, slopping a pitcher of milk on the table. She loped across the kitchen, opened the door to the back stairs, and hollered up, "Come an' git it!"

On the way to Charlie's house with the marbles bag in his pocket, Luke was excited about what he had heard at Milligan's Store. He had a fantastic plan, and he could hardly wait to tell Charlie. By the time he reached Charlie's, he was so excited that he had trouble swallowing the milk that Mrs. Tatum made him drink while he waited for Charlie to finish his breakfast of bacon and eggs, biscuits dripping molasses, and milk.

"Now you just drink that down, young man," said Mrs. Tatum. "Them bones of yours are growin' so fast, you need all the milk you can get."

When they were finally on the road to school, and a safe distance from the house, Luke told Charlie about the cave-in, or at least *most* of what Herb Norris had said. He drew Charlie off to the side of the road, into a patch of alders. Looking around suspiciously, he dug into his pocket and brought out the marbles bag.

"You know what this is?" Luke asked, with a swagger in his voice.

"Yeah. It's a bag of marbles," Charlie answered, unimpressed.

"Guess again, my friend. This ain't no bag of marbles."

"Then what the heck is it?" Charlie snapped.

With a flourish, Luke pulled the drawstring and dumped out several small white fragments of ore into the palm of his hand. The ore was peppered with tiny gold nuggets.

Charlie's eyes popped. He had seen nuggets before—his father and some friends had prospected in the mine years ago and had "souvenirs" to show for it—but Charlie had never seen *so much* raw gold before in his life.

"Where'd you get that? You musta stole it. I'll bet that you stole it!"

"No, I didn't steal it. I prospected for it. I prospected for it in the mine," Luke replied proudly.

"When?" demanded Charlie, feeling slighted at being left out of even one of Luke's adventures.

"Last summer. I made a few trips into the mine with a couple friends, and we prospected for it. This was my share."

"Damn. That's a lot of gold, Luke. What's it worth?"

"It's worth a lot. I been savin' it."

"So what are you gettin' at?"

"What I'm gettin' at, dummy, is that Mr. Norris's cave-in prob'ly uncovered untapped territory for huntin' nuggets."

Luke waited for an excited reaction, but Charlie only shifted his weight.

"Well, do you know what that means?" asked Luke.

"Yeah. It means stay outta the mine."

Luke rolled his eyes heavenward. "You know what's wrong with you, Charlie Tatum? You got no imagination whatsoever. You're a-scared of your own shadow. Now, do you wanna go prospectin' or not?"

Charlie had never been in the mine, and even talking about it made him uneasy. He knew that Luke's plan would get him into trouble. He also knew that Luke would talk him into it. Luke could talk Charlie into almost anything.

"Oh, I don't know, Luke," Charlie mumbled feebly.

"There ain't nothin' to worry about, Charlie. I can find my way blindfolded to the sinkhole. If we just follow the old ore-car tracks, we'll be fine," Luke said with confidence.

Luke was familiar with the sinkhole. He and two other boys had gone swimming in it many times. The place was lonely, the water cold and murky green. No matter how deep they dived, they had never touched or even seen the bottom. Luke hadn't admitted to his hooky-playing friends that the sinkhole gave him the creeps. He imagined something deep in the water, staring up at them with bulging black eyes, waiting to pull them down. What if Old Maud, metamorphosed into a giant eel, wound herself around their legs and dragged them, struggling, deep down through the murky depths? If Luke was in the water when these images crossed his mind, he'd kick furiously to the bank and pull his body quickly from the dark pool.

Luke knew that the mine was Old Maud's territory. The possibility of sighting her was a constant source of wariness. But at the same time he felt a heightened sense of adventure with each forbidden trip into the mine. Excited by his plan, he shrugged aside these disturbing thoughts. As his persuasive argument with Charlie continued, he also convinced himself that, with or without Charlie, he was going prospecting in the mine the very next weekend.

"I've got it all worked out," he said. "I'm headin' out first light on Saturday mornin', and I'll be back before suppertime. I've got a saddlebag packed with everything I need—food, water, rope, a hand pick for diggin', and a flashlight with brand-new batteries."

Actually, Luke hadn't yet assembled any of these items. He was organizing the expedition as he went along. His show of confidence finally persuaded Charlie.

"All right. I'll go, but if my folks find out, they'll skin me alive," he said. Then he paused. "Is Silky goin'? If Silky's goin', count me out."

"No, Silky ain't goin'. She knows nothin' about this prospectin' expedition."

With Charlie's principal condition met, he asked, "How much gold do you think we'll find?"

Luke smiled to himself. "Prob'ly hundreds of dollars worth, maybe thousands. Your folks' eyes will pop when they see all them nuggets."

Thirteen

"I don't think we should trust Herb with our secret. It's too risky," said Nathan Lightfoot at supper that night. "He thinks we're after some herbs or a potion from Maud. Why don't we just go along with his notion?"

"You're right," said Big John, stroking his chin. "What if Maud wants to stay where she is? She has a right to do whatever she wants. We can't force her to come live with us. If the village finds out who she is before we've had a chance to talk with her, there'll be questions we can't answer."

"I agree, Father," said Billy. "We'll just have to think of a good reason for needing one of Maud's potions."

Big John's eyes grew worried. He spoke as though thinking aloud. "Yes. They'll want to pry into our family's history. They'll want to know how she escaped the fire. You can't blame them for being curious. We have the same questions, but her privacy must be respected. They'll be coming around to get a closer look. How can we protect her from nosy neighbors? If Maud comes down from the mine, she must do so on her own terms." Big John looked from face to face around the table. These were problems and questions none of them had considered.

~ ~ ~

Having decided not to give Herb advance notice about their rendezvous with Maud, Big John and Johnny arrived at Herb's door on Sunday morning at sunup. They stood on the threshold a moment before knocking.

"Are you ready, Johnny?" asked Big John.

"I'm ready, Grandfather."

Big John knocked heavily on the door.

Startled by the sound, Herb Norris jumped out of bed. For a moment he reeled from confusion and dizziness. With the next knock, he hurried down the stairs, threw open the door, and blinked at his visitors.

"Herb," said Big John, drawing himself up to his full six-plus feet. "I must ask you to open the gate. We have had news from Old Maud, as you know. She has a potion that we desperately need for my son's wife, Mary. We can't wait any longer. Mary must not lose this baby if Old Maud can help us."

Poor Herb looked bewildered. In his half-conscious state, he only partially understood what Big John was saying. Could they be asking him to compromise his responsibilities and jeopardize his job?

"I can't do it, Big John. I'm responsible for the safety of this community. I can't let you into the mine."

"I'm only asking that you allow us to meet Old Maud at the clearing at the top of Mine Hill. Those were her instructions. I can't believe that you would accept responsibility for the death of an unborn child to save your job."

"Please, Mr. Norris, open the gate," said Johnny.

Herb finally understood the significance of their request. "I'll drive you in my pickup to the top of the clearing. Wait for me at the gate." He turned back into the house to dress.

At the top of the hill, Herb suggested he wait with them in case Old Maud didn't come, but they insisted they wait alone. They promised that if she didn't appear in a reasonable length of time, they would come back down so he could relock the gate.

Big John and Johnny didn't have long to wait. The sun was full up when, peering down the length of the ore-car tracks, Big John spied a small, bent figure slowly approaching the clearing.

He strained forward, shading his eyes against the sun, and prepared himself for his face-to-face encounter with his cousin.
Chum could hardly restrain himself.

As she came closer, Maud slowed her steps along the tracks..
She hesitated for a second, perhaps unsure of how she should greet
her cousin. Then, as they watched, she lifted her chin, squared her
shoulders as best she could, and walked proudly toward them.

Chum broke away and raced toward her, barking and wagging
his tail. Johnny hung back, feeling shy and unsure after so long a
separation. When Maud stopped to pet Chum so enthusiastically,
Johnny ran to her side and motioned to his grandfather.

Big John walked slowly toward Maud, his eyes riveted on her
face. Her appearance did, indeed, shock him at first. He had never
seen a face so disfigured, but its expression touched him. That one
blue eye revealed the strong, proud spirit within her pathetic, mis-
shapen body. Big John was profoundly moved. How this poor creature standing before him could be so terribly maligned was the
cruelest injustice. Yet it was not pity that he felt. There was dignity
in the way she held her head, and a certain defiance in her direct
gaze. He was happy and excited about their meeting, and he hoped
that she could see it in his expression.

When they stood facing each other, he opened his arms to
her. She hesitated a moment, then stepped into his embrace.

Her body was solid and strong, unlike the frail, birdlike
skeletons of so many of his brittle, old kinfolk. He held her close.

After a moment, he stepped back and held Maud at arm's
length. "Today is one of the happiest days of my life," he said. "I
hope that today will be the beginning of a new life for us both.
Because the same blood runs in our veins, what is mine is yours."

"I have waited most of my life for this day," said Maud.
"They have made it possible." She gestured toward Johnny and
Chum. "Please come with me now, Cousin," she said. "We will
talk. I have much to tell you. Walk directly behind me on the
tracks. Don't stray. Here is a short rope for the dog, Johnny. Keep
him close."

Maud led the way to her little cabin. From time to time, she
turned to make sure that Big John was keeping up. They said
nothing to each other on the way. In some places, the rails and

what remained of the ties were under water, and they had to balance themselves on the rails for a few feet to cross. Big John marveled at Maud's agility, whereas he had to be helped by his grandson to make the crossing safely.

Johnny was completely unfamiliar with this part of the mine. The topography was very different from the path he had taken from Cobequid Road with Chum. It was flatter, and there were no bushes or trees whatsoever, only the tracks. They passed the sinkhole, now as big as a lake, and the black, open pit of the recent cave-in that Herb Norris had described. The loneliness of the place was oppressive, and Johnny was glad he wasn't alone. There was a damp and musty smell in the air despite the bright sunshine. He realized the great danger in being in the mine area without a skilled guide such as Maud.

"Are you tired, Cousin? Shall we stop to rest?" Maud turned and called back to Big John. "It is not much farther."

Johnny was surprised that his grandfather was able to keep up. He seemed rejuvenated and eager, even younger.

"No," Big John replied. "We have a great deal to say in very little time. We must hurry."

He was concerned that Herb Norris would become alarmed and perhaps suspicious if they were not back at the clearing within a reasonable time.

Finally, Johnny recognized the path between Maud's cabin and the pit he had fallen into. There were the charred remains from his wood fire. Let off the leash, Chum raced ahead to the open, roofless shaft between the great rocks that led to Maud's cabin. He barked at them to hurry.

Johnny's thoughts returned to his frightening experience the first night he had traveled this path with his wounded dog to Maud's cabin, comparing that trip to the now-familiar way that seemed shorter and easier to follow each time he walked it. Everything looked the same inside the cabin. He was glad to be there again, and under more positive circumstances. Chum seemed completely at home. He barked in recognition of the crow roosting on the shelf behind the stove.

"I could fetch water for tea, Maud," said Johnny, glancing at his grandfather, proud of his familiarity with the place.

"Yes," said Maud, handing him the kettle from the stove.

Johnny disappeared through the back door, out to the well.

"Your grandson is very brave. He is a sensitive and kind young man. You must be very proud of him."

"He is, indeed. And we *are* proud of him," said Big John. "You saved his life, but we were still afraid for him when he came to you with the dog. We were ignorant. Johnny, however, believed in you from the beginning."

Maud settled herself in her chair beside the stove. Big John took the birch twig stool. She opened the door of the woodstove and shoved a large tree knot into the embers. Chum circled a space at Maud' feet, curled up, and went to sleep.

Johnny returned from the well and placed the kettle of water on the stove. He folded his long legs to sit on the floor in front of his grandfather. He had looked forward to this meeting all winter. With Big John there and Maud firmly established as their cousin, he felt a warm family closeness that seemed almost as comfortable as being in his own home.

"Where shall I begin?" asked Maud.

"Wherever you feel the need," answered Big John.

"What I'm about to tell you happened a lifetime ago," Maud began. "But I remember it as vividly as if it were yesterday. To me, it was truly the only significant time in my life—a life much longer than I expected, or wanted.

"I was sixteen years old and engaged to be married. I had a wonderful life with two doting parents, and a young man, Emile, who loved me and wanted to make a good life for us both. He worked hard in the mine. I worried about him constantly. He never learned to read and write, and so he went to school with the younger children of the village whenever he had time from work. He studied for hours into the night. He wanted to be a teacher, as I did. But he was much smarter than I, and children took to him so naturally.

"Emile's parents were against us from the start. They knew that my mother was Micmac. They criticized her for running a tavern. She was loose and drunken, they said. They warned Emile that I would bring him nothing but grief, that I was wild, a half-breed, and stupid. They tried to poison Emile's mind against me with these accusations. They made his life so miserable that he asked me to elope with him, which I agreed to do. We were to leave for Windsor Junction in a week and take the train to Digby. We had saved a little money, and planned to start a new life there."

Here she paused in her story and bowed her head. Big John and Johnny said nothing, but waited quietly for her to continue.

"It was the night before our departure," Maud said with such sadness in her voice that Big John felt he must spare her the agony of telling her story. Before he could choose the right words, however, Maud continued.

"My mother watched me skip around my room with happiness as I packed my things. My parents loved Emile. They were very happy about our marriage, although disappointed that they could not be with us. They knew that Emile's father would ruin a wedding ceremony at home among our family and friends.

"That night, my father was working in the tavern. Mother and I were in my room upstairs. It was almost closing time when we heard a ruckus from the tavern. There were loud voices, cursing, and the sounds of a scuffle. We were frightened. There had never been a fight in our tavern before. 'Stay here,' Mother said. 'Do not come down, no matter what.' She ran downstairs and reached the tavern just as Emile's father, Gene Trudeau, crashed through the front door and tumbled onto the road. I ran to my open window and looked out, horrified. Emile's father was sprawled in the middle of the road. I could see that he was bleeding from the nose and mouth. Father stood over him, fists clenched. I heard his voice tremble with his words: 'If you ever step foot in my tavern again, Trudeau, I swear I'll kill you.'

"Trudeau crawled away from Father, got to his feet, and stumbled down the road. While he was still within earshot, he turned and shouted, 'You just keep that half-breed daughter of yours away from my son.'

"Mother returned to my room and found me paralyzed with fear. Father followed, sat down beside me, and stroked my hair. His lip was cut and swollen, and a blue lump was forming under his right eye. The sight of him shocked me even further. 'Trudeau insulted you and your mother,' he said to me in French. 'I am sorry I had to do what I did. I know what you are thinking, Maud. Don't worry about Emile, my darling. He'll come for you tomorrow night.'"

Maud paused in her story to pour hot water over the herbs in three tin cups. She quietly handed one to Big John and another to Johnny, then took hers and sat back down.

"I worried about Emile that night and cried myself to sleep. My dreams were troubled, and I felt hot and feverish. I don't know what time it was when I was awakened by mother's screams outside my bedroom door. I thought I was having a horrible nightmare. I was confused when I couldn't see anything but thick smoke. I tried to reach my bedroom door when Father suddenly appeared beside me. He pulled me into the hallway, where Mother was choking and coughing, clutching our family Bible. Father forced us to the floor, and shouted something to Mother. The smell of kerosene was very strong. I turned around and saw the flames roaring up the front staircase from the tavern, blocking our escape."

Maud became more agitated as she spoke. Her words came fast, and her breathing grew heavy. She closed her eye and rocked herself, her hands clenched tightly around her cup. Big John sat motionless. Johnny's heart was pounding.

"We were gasping for air as Father dragged Mother and me down the narrow back stairs. As we reached the hallway to the back door, the flames leaped from the side door of the tavern and drove us back. Father pushed the heavy door closed, giving us some relief from the intense heat. I could barely see him through the smoke as he groped on the floor on his hands and knees, looking for something. Just then, an explosion inside the tavern blew the door off its hinges. The heat from the flames washed over me and burned into my throat. The tavern was now completely engulfed. Flaming beams hung from the ceiling where the floor above had collapsed. At last Father found what he was looking for: the ring on the trapdoor to the root cellar.

"He pulled open the door and dangled me down until my feet reached a rung of the ladder. My eyes stung, and I couldn't see in the darkness, but I felt my way down the ladder to the bottom rung and stumbled over some barrels. I heard my mother drop from the ladder behind me. Suddenly, there was another explosion, and a huge fireball shot through the trapdoor opening, knocking us both down. I heard Mother call to Father. He had not come through the trapdoor. Mother shoved the Bible into my arms and shouted, 'Run, Maud! Run and don't look back.' She started back up the ladder and disappeared into the heavy smoke. I tried to follow, but flames drove me back. I ran as fast as I could through the adjoining passage to the mine. As I ran, I heard the floor collapse and saw the flames shoot through the tunnel behind me."

She paused. Moisture glistened on her brow. In a low, husky voice, she said, "When I looked back, I knew my parents were gone."

Maud's shoulders sagged with grief. She rolled her head back and uttered a long, mournful cry. It was like the cry of a wounded animal facing death alone in the wilderness. It echoed through the cabin, and into the little canyon behind, through the solitary years of a life without loved ones. It hung in the trees of the forest, and followed the howling wind to the graves of her ancestors. It was the voice of a mourning Micmac, full of pain, suffering, and loss.

Big John waited in stunned silence. He understood her profound sorrowful lament, and the relief he knew it would bring her.

Johnny had never heard a more mournful sound. He rose and gently took the cup from Maud's hands. He held them between his own hands and knelt beside her. Tears streamed down the right side of her face, and he offered his folded handkerchief. Her wailing finally trailed off to wracking sobs. He placed the cup of soothing tea back into her hands. Maud took a sip and touched Johnny's face.

When she had quieted herself, she continued her story.

"I ran through the darkness to a connecting tunnel from the cellar into the mine. It was pitch black, but I knew it so well that I could grope my way along the walls and find the tunnel to the main chamber. I walked for a very long time until I finally came to the end of the tunnel and into the night. It was raining. I remember holding something in my arms that I could not seem to let go. I walked through the woods and over the fields all the rest of that night and the next day. I must have been in shock, because I remember very little of my journey. Before darkness fell the following night, I found myself at my father's brother's house. It was a miracle.

"I lay bandaged for weeks. The doctor couldn't save my eye. When the bandages came off, I asked for a mirror. My uncle refused, but I found one in Aunt Jane's dresser drawer. I knew I was badly burned, but I was not prepared for the horror that stared back at me when I had the courage to look. I thought of Emile. I wanted to die, because I realized I could never see him again.

"Uncle Jacques and Aunt Jane were good to me and took care of me. They told me what happened after the fire. I made them promise to tell no one that I had escaped. There was a funeral service for my parents, but I would not leave my room. I hid myself away in that room for nine years. After Aunt Jane passed away, I went back to the mine and watched Beaver Creek from a hiding place, hoping to see Emile. I didn't know he had died mysteriously eight years before.

"Uncle Jacques helped me move the assayer's cabin to this spot. Before he died, he told me that the Lightfoot family were relatives of my mother. He pointed out your farm, and I watched your children and your children's children grow. When the wind was right, I could hear their voices carry from below. I learned their names, and wrote each one in my family Bible."

Big John rose stiffly from the stool, walked to the little window, and looked out. It was several minutes before he could trust himself to speak.

"It's an incredible story, Maud, a most incredibly *tragic* story. A stronger, more courageous woman I have never known. Had you come to us sooner, and told us who you were . . . ."

Maud shook her head and put a hand on Johnny's shoulder. "Had Johnny not recognized the photographs—one mine, the other yours—we would not be together here today. I never intended to make my identity known to anyone."

"I'm astonished that you survived alone all these years," said Big John. "How did you keep clothes on your back, food on the table, and maintain this little house? How could you do all these things without some kind of personal contact, someone to help you? Surely you needed shoes, needles, thread, pots in which to cook your food, these very cups for tea."

"I have not seen my face in a mirror for more than forty years. I don't fully remember how I look. I know I've grown careless in my old age. I'm reminded of my ugliness only when I come upon an unsuspecting hunter in the woods or near the mine. Children run screaming if I pass their homes at twilight. As for your other question, I hunt and pick berries, and I grow my own vegetables. For my other simple needs, there is a peddler who comes through Windsor Junction from time to time. He is probably as ugly as I, and he trades with me."

"But what do you use for money?"

"The peddler has a taste for rabbit, but I also have gold," said Maud innocently.

Big John remembered Herb's passing remark about gold nuggets in exchange for gifts of food. He marveled at his cousin's remarkable resourcefulness and independence.

Johnny sat silently, waiting for his grandfather to approach the main reason for their visit. He cleared his throat as a signal.

Big John smiled and held out his hands. "Cousin Maud, you have lived alone too long, and it is no longer necessary for you to do that. We would be honored to have you come live with us. We want you to share in our lives and good fortune, and to lend us some of your strength and wisdom. We will protect you, and care for you, and give you the kind of life your parents wanted for you. It would make us all very happy. You will be a member of our village as well as our family. Will you consider our offer?"

After a long pause, Maud said, "I am honored that you would want me. Long ago I yearned to be with my own people, that I might walk among them and be one of them again. But I am an old woman now, and my life in the mine is the only life I know. I thank you for your kind invitation, Cousin. I will think on it."

She rose from her chair, walked to the shelf, and held out a hand to the crow. It squawked once, and curled its dark claws around her fingers.

"Crow and I will see you back to the clearing," she said.

"No, Maud," said Big John. "We'll retrace our steps to the tracks. There's no need for you to trouble yourself."

Big John was crestfallen, but he felt the need to press. "When will we know your answer?" he asked gently.

"Soon," she replied. "I will send word soon."

Johnny's heart sank as they said good-bye to Maud once more. "She'll never leave," he said sadly to his grandfather on their way back. "She'll die right here in the mine."

Fourteen

Luke finally admitted to Charlie that they were lost. Charlie was hungry and scared. He tried desperately not to cry, but he felt hot tears run down his cheeks. Luke sat beside him and rummaged through his saddlebag for a candy bar. They had walked through a maze of dark tunnels for hours until the batteries in the flashlight grew weak. They had just sat down to rest when Luke snapped off the flashlight.

"Hey, what're you doin'? Turn that light back on," demanded Charlie, his panic piercing the darkness.

"We got to save the batteries," Luke said flatly.

Early that morning they had scrambled down the side of the open pit of the latest cave-in and worked their way into the new mouth of the part of the tunnel that was still intact. Intent in their search for gold, they had failed to notice a nearby branching of the main chamber.

The boys had worked their way farther into this new tunnel until the light began to fade from the entrance. Luke proudly produced his new flashlight, and continued tapping the tunnel walls with the pick, loosening the rock and handing it to Charlie to examine for nuggets.

Charlie had grown tired of their prospecting game after a few hours and began to complain. They had very little to show for their work and time spent.

"C'mon, Luke. It's gettin' late. What time is it anyway?"

Luke looked up from his tapping. "I don't have a watch, but I know it ain't late. We just ate, and that was noontime."

"Yeah, but my stomach's tellin' me it's almost suppertime. We better start back."

"Okay, okay. Just hold the light here 'til I loosen this very promisin' lookin' chunk."

When they had finally pried out the rock, they examined it carefully and found a good-size nugget in the whitish vein on the underside. In their excitement they didn't notice a tiny trickle of water oozing from a narrow crack under the rock that they had just extracted from the wall. Babbling enthusiastically over their find, they mistakenly turned left and continued farther into the new tunnel.

They had walked only a few minutes when Charlie stopped suddenly and said, "There wasn't any water on the ground when we came in here. And we're walkin' on bare rock now. We're goin' the wrong way, Luke."

"You're right," Luke said, looking behind. "Now, don't panic. We'll just go the other way. When we turn the corner up there, we'll see daylight. Come on."

Carrying the saddlebag over one shoulder, Charlie walked behind Luke, who shined the flashlight in the dark tunnel. The beam of light ran upward and along the side walls of the tunnel, where the timbers showed patches of wetness. Somewhere from the twisting corridors came the sound of slowly dripping water— *plink, plink, plink.*

The boys turned the corner and walked another twenty yards. There were no tracks on the floor of the tunnel—theirs or anyone else's. Charlie said nothing. He tried to swallow the lump of fear growing in his throat. His confidence fading, Luke hoped he could keep his composure for Charlie's sake.

Fifteen

Tom Graywolf sat alone at his kitchen table and listened to the ticking of the clock. Esther and the boys were at home and accounted for—all except Luke. It was Saturday night at half-past nine when Tom heard a timid rapping on the door.

"What's he knockin' on his own door for?" Tom grumbled, grabbing the lamp from the middle of the table. "Scared of the lickin' he's gonna get, I s'pose." He yanked the door open expecting to see Luke's hangdog expression. Instead, the lamplight fell on the grave faces of Jack and Elma Tatum.

"Evenin', Tom," said Jack. "Is my boy here with your boy?"

"Your boy ain't here, and my boy ain't here neither."

Elma Tatum's hand flew to her mouth, stifling a cry.

"Your boy Luke came to the house early this mornin' and picked up Charlie," said Jack. "They said they was goin' fishin' . . . Come to think of it, I didn't see no fishin' pole. But I s'pose that ain't unusual. Luke coulda had fishin' line in his saddlebag," Jack added cautiously. "Leastwise, Charlie didn't come home for supper, and that ain't like him."

"Are you signifyin' that my boy Luke is to blame for your boy stayin' out this late?" asked Graywolf threateningly.

"I ain't signifyin' nothin, Tom," said Jack. "I'm just lookin' for my boy, and I thought he might be here with Luke."

"Well, he ain't. I don't know where they are," said Graywolf, concern softening his expression. He looked back at the clock.

"It ain't that late yet. Don't worry. They know how to swim if they fell in. Besides, the creek ain't no deeper than three feet at the most. When Luke comes home, I'll give *him* a lickin', and if Charlie's with him, I'll bring him home myself by the scruff of the neck."

Gathering her jacket closer around her, Elma turned to go. Jack looked up at Graywolf and said seriously, "Charlie's my only son, Tom. He ain't never stayed out like this before."

"Neither's Luke," answered Graywolf.

Graywolf closed the door, sat down at the table, and remembered what Jack had said about the saddlebag. He felt a nagging uneasiness connected to it. Would Luke be running away from home just like Tom himself had done at exactly the same age? Tom was determined to wait up all night if he had to, until Luke came home.

Graywolf waited, but Luke didn't come home.

As soon as it was light enough, he left the house and headed for the creek. He needed to see for himself whether the boys had been there. He studied the surface of the narrow dirt road leading to the creek, looking for tracks. From the end of the road at the water's edge, he walked upstream and downstream along the muddy bank. There were only tracks of animals that had come to drink at sundown the evening before. He waded to the other side of the stream. Nothing. The boys had not been fishing in the creek.

Graywolf walked to the Tatums' house. They, too, hadn't slept all night. Elma's eyes were red and swollen from crying.

"We're goin' to need help to look for the boys," Graywolf said. "I'm goin' up to the lumber camp to get my men. Jack, you go to Milligan's Store. By noon today, we should have a search party ready to go. Now, don't you worry none, Elma. We'll find 'em."

Later that morning, more than a dozen farmers gathered at Milligan's Store for a search party. Jack Tatum was there with Elma, who wept anew each time Charlie's name was mentioned.

Ideas were exchanged as to where the boys might be. Were they lost in the woods, kidnapped by gypsies? Had they run away? When all was said and done, it was the consensus that Old Maud, without a doubt, had something to do with the boys' disappearance.

Just after noon, Graywolf arrived at Milligan's Store with his men on a flatbed truck from the lumber camp. They were a young, boisterous bunch from the next county, more interested in the extra day's pay that Graywolf had offered than any real concern for the missing boys.

The lumbermen circulated among the farmers, listening to accusations against Old Maud and adding their own prejudices and prejudgments to the growing suspicions against her. A flask of whiskey, passed from man to man, flashed in the sun. Milligan grew nervous behind his store counter, and motioned for Graywolf to follow him into the back room.

"Listen, Tom," he said timidly. "I don't want no trouble around here. I don't think it was a good idea bringin' in these outsiders from the camp. We can handle this thing ourselves. They could get out of hand if we're not careful. They're already talkin' about goin' into the mine after Old Maud."

"Aw, these farmers around here are old women," scoffed Graywolf. "My men'll do what *I* tell 'em," he growled. "I'm takin' half of 'em up to Windsor Junction, and we'll work our way back through the west woods. I have a notion where the boys went. I think Luke's runnin' away from home, and takin' the Tatum boy with him. They're prob'ly on their way to the Junction to hop a boxcar," he said, casually referring to his own past history as though it were normal behavior for every boy of Luke and Charlie's age.

Graywolf went outside and spoke to Jack Tatum.

"Jack, you and your men comb the woods to the east and around Loon Lake. Then, head south alongside the railroad tracks back to Larson's farm. Get some tin cans or somethin' to beat on constant that the boys might hear. Firin' shots won't do no good—

in the woods, you can't tell what direction they're comin' from. Take a couple of good trackin' dogs. We're goin' up to the Junction and work our way west, then south. That way we'll make a complete circle around the mine. I know some men in the hobo camp at the Junction who mighta seen the boys."

Jack was puzzled. "But the boys know their way home from the Junction." He paused as fear flickered in his eyes. "You don't think some hobo . . ."

"What I think is, the boys might try to hop a boxcar west," said Graywolf, his eyes distant, remembering his long and lonely flight from an abusive home life many years ago.

"You mean runnin' away from home? But, why . . .?"

"We don't have time for all that now, Jack. I'm leavin' half my men with you. Me and the other half will meet you and your boys back at the south side of the mine at Larson's farm at sundown. If we're lucky, we'll have Luke and Charlie in tow."

Graywolf turned and called to his lumberjack gang, who climbed, yelling and laughing, onto the back of the truck. They were over the hill and gone before Jack Tatum, with a puzzled expression, gathered his farmer friends together. Heartsick and worried, he asked himself why his Charlie would run away from home.

"Well, come on, men," yelled a pock-faced lumberjack from Graywolf's camp. Let's go find them boys."

As soon as they were gone, Milligan saddled up and rode out to Herb Norris's gatehouse.

Herb had been listening to his radio on Sunday afternoon. The announcer had just reported strong winds and thunderstorms moving northwest off the Atlantic when Herb heard Milligan call from out on the road. He opened the door, and was surprised to see Milligan on horseback.

"Where's your Ford, Milligan? Come on in and have some coffee."

"My car's broke down, and I don't have time for no coffee. Got to get back to the store. I come to tell you that Tom Graywolf's boy Luke, and Jack Tatum's Charlie, turned up missin' last night. About an hour ago Jack took Max, the Callahan brothers,

Cyril, and some of the other boys, includin' ten of Graywolf's lumbermen, on a search party into the woods hereabouts. Graywolf took the other ten and went west in the opposite direction. Before they left my place, that rowdy bunch from Graywolf's camp started drinkin', and they were talkin' about Old Maud takin' the two boys, and how they was goin' into the mine after her."

Milligan took a breath. "I'm tellin' you, Herb, I see trouble comin'."

"Slow down, slow down," said Herb, somewhat confused. "Are the boys in the mine?"

"Nobody knows. They're searchin' the woods. Graywolf thinks they're on their way to the Junction, runnin' away from home. The two search parties are s'posed to meet back at Ralph Larson's place at sundown, one way or the other. If they don't find the boys in the woods, they're goin' into the mine, Herb. I just know it."

"They won't get past my gate, and they'd be fools to try any other route. A storm is heading this way, and it'll be dark early. Graywolf knows about the cave-ins. His men won't go into the mine tonight in the storm."

"Even Graywolf can't control twenty drunken lumberjacks, Herb. I seen it happen before, up the line a few years ago. A bunch of them galoots got crazy drunk and tore the town apart—killed two people. I don't want that to happen here." Milligan glanced behind him. "I gotta get back."

Herb had heard that story—how a drunken mob had formed to spring a lumberjack buddy out of the town lockup. He knew that Milligan wasn't a man to worry unnecessarily or to scare easily. Herb immediately sized up the situation and realized what he had to do.

"Do me a favor," Herb called after him. "On your way back, stop at the Lightfoot farm and tell them what's going on. I might need some help keeping the gate tonight."

Milligan waved and trotted off down Cobequid Road.

Herb went back inside, took his rifle down from its rack above the door, found a box of shells, and turned up the volume on the radio.

~ ~ ~

Graywolf drove the flatbed truck at breakneck speed up Cobequid Road. Less than a quarter mile from the Windsor Junction railroad crossing, he turned west onto a deeply rutted dirt road running parallel to the tracks. The men on the back of the truck, hanging on to the vehicle's log chains, laughed drunkenly as they were bounced about on the truck bed. At the Junction, Graywolf observed switching crews and engines shunting boxcars and oil cars from one track to another. Loaded coal cars sat on idle tracks at a distance from the working engines. Ragged men—hobos—climbed the laddered sides of the cars and tossed large lumps of coal down onto the embankment. Their companions on the ground stuffed the coal into burlap sacks, and headed back into the woods with loads of the fuel for their campfires.

Graywolf drove on until the road veered away from the tracks and headed deeper into the woods. He slowed, peering through the trees. Several old car wrecks and truck bodies lay scattered about. Campfires were being tended by wretched, bearded men in dark overcoats and battered felt hats. Graywolf could see them pacing back and forth, their boots patched with strips and circles cut from old tire tubes. Each of the cars, the bare wheels raised on blocks, had a number painted on its battered door like room numbers in a hotel.

Graywolf was searching for someone in particular. Straining to see through his dirty windshield, he approached a beat-up tractor-trailer body attached to a tattered green tent. Apparently customized to accommodate a more permanent resident, this trailer stood apart from the other shelters. There were steps leading to a door on the side of the trailer facing the road. The door's tarpaper skin displayed a fancy pattern of flathead nails. A dingy bed sheet hung from a window, which had been cut out and fitted with a large pane of glass. A plume of black smoke rose from a galvanized stovepipe sticking up through the patched roof. A roaring fire fed by pieces of car batteries burned in front of the attached tent, and through its open flaps Graywolf saw a long table where a few men sat playing cards.

Graywolf drove his truck a few feet beyond the tent, sounded the horn, and waited. A dog barked from inside the trailer body. Finally, a gray-haired bearded man appeared at the door, quickly closing it behind him to keep the dog from escaping. The man was gaunt and tall, and his flesh appeared an unhealthy gray-brown, a color matching his clothing. Sunken eyes glared like glass beads from his wizened face.

Ordering his men on the flatbed to "stay put," Graywolf got out of the truck. He picked his way through rusty car parts, old tires, orange crates, and broken bottles to where the man stood above him on the top step.

"Hello, Jake. Been a long time. It's me, Tom Graywolf. How you been keepin'?"

Shading his eyes from the sun, Jake squinted at Graywolf. He studied him a moment, then let out a whoop.

"Tom Graywolf, you stinkin' polecat! I remember now. You owe me two bucks, you miserable bum."

Jake hobbled down the steps with open arms and hugged his old friend. Graywolf grabbed Jake in a bear hug and lifted him clear off the ground, both men hooting and howling with laughter.

The two men reminisced about their early hobo adventures until Graywolf, uneasy with the passing time, stated his mission to Jake's camp. He described Luke and Charlie, and the circumstances of their disappearance. He explained how the search party had been organized. He expressed his concerns that Luke, carrying a saddlebag, might be running away from home.

"I come to ask if you'd seen my boy."

"Your boy ain't been through here, Graywolf. I know every man and boy who's been through this camp for the past thirty years. I know when every boxcar leaves the Junction, where it's goin' and who's in it. When a train pulls in from out west, I got ways of knowin' who jumps off in the dark. This is the end of the line, or the beginnin', dependin' on your point of view. I got me a real good setup here."

"But what about the railroad authorities, the security police?" asked Graywolf.

"Railroad authorities can't touch me. I own the land—bought it fair and square from a farmer who got tired of milkin' cows. Every mother's son down on his luck who passes through my camp pays me a small fee, sometimes only a thin dime. It ain't much, but it puts food on the table. I put 'em up for a night or two in my 'bedroom cars,' feed 'em good next mornin', give 'em hot water to shave and wash if they're so inclined, and send 'em on their way. Sometimes a job comes along that one of the young fellers might be good at," Jake said smiling, proud of his hobo community. "Wish we had a hobo camp like this when we was ridin' the rails."

Graywolf reflected on those hard and lonely times. He admired Jake's compassion and empathy for these less fortunate men. Having run away from a bad experience in an orphanage upriver, Jake never complained about his lot in life; he always had a happy-go-lucky attitude and made the best of what he had. Graywolf wondered how Jake turned out the way he did, and wished that he, too, had grown up to be a different kind of person, one not so embittered and harsh. But now he had a job to do, and he pushed these thoughts from his mind.

Graywolf told Jake about the stories that had spread through Beaver Creek—of an eccentric old woman who had been troubling the townspeople for years, and who they felt had something to do with the disappearance of the boys.

"She's called Old Maud, a witch, a dangerous old woman who practices black magic." Graywolf pointed to the men on the flatbed truck. "Me and my men are prepared to go into the mine where she lives if we have to."

Jake was incredulous. "Old Maud?" he exclaimed. "You can't be serious. I know Maud. She's been tradin' for years with Mr. Addis, the peddler who comes through here. Maud's no witch! She's helped me nurse sick men who fell out of boxcars with pneumonia, tuberculosis, and broken bones. Maud is my friend, and an angel to the poor souls who need her help. She ain't harmed them boys, Graywolf. I'll bet you the two bucks you owe me. The whole idea is ridiculous," he scoffed.

Graywolf suddenly seemed embarrassed and uneasy. He regretted mentioning Old Maud's name in such offensive terms, contrary to his friend's high opinion of her. He had exposed his ignorant superstitions to Jake, who was obviously above all that. What was worse, he had implied that his own son, Luke, had reasons for running away from home. With deep feelings of remorse, Graywolf said good-bye to Jake, and promised to visit again as soon as his present troubles were over. He reached into his pocket and brought out two one dollar bills and handed them to his friend. Jake smiled, wished him luck, and said he was confident that the boys would be found unharmed.

When Graywolf returned to the truck, three hobos were standing around trading cigarettes for whiskey with some of the lumbermen. They bickered and argued until a punch was thrown just as Graywolf gave a shrill whistle. The men hardly had time to jump back on the truck before Graywolf roared away. They drove southwest, heading toward the mine. When they arrived at the crossroads where Graywolf had planned to begin the search, the men jumped down from the truck and were ordered to spread out and comb the woods. Having sobered up sufficiently, Jean-Paul Laval was chosen to drive the truck back to Larson's farm, where they would rejoin the others at sundown.

Sixteen

Maud watched from her window until Big John and Johnny disappeared at the end of her canyon. She sighed, still feeling the warmth and pleasure of their touch. Big John had a kind and generous heart. He was sincere, and he had not recoiled from holding her in his arms. It had been so many years since she had been touched by another human being—not since her Uncle Jacques died holding her hand.

Maud opened the door of her bedchamber and sat on the bed of skins. She lit the candle on the bedside box, then placed her family Bible on her lap and opened it. She read the names recorded there, some she had long forgotten. She placed her fingers lovingly on her parents' names, then on the names of the Lightfoot family. The name of her mother's nephew, John Victor Lightfoot—Big John—had been written in her mother's hand. Years later, Maud herself had inscribed the names of Big John's two sons, Nathan and William, and the names of Nathan's children with their approximate dates of birth.

Maud carefully turned the pages of the Bible to the photographs of her parents and members of her family long since dead and gone. There was no likeness of her beloved Emile, but she didn't need one to remember his handsome face and gentle ways.

In exactly the middle of the book, the center of the remaining pages had been skillfully cut out in a three-inch square, and in the hollow lay two plump rectangular cotton bags. The four edges of each bag had been carefully sewn together in the shape of tiny pillows by Maud's mother, and contained gold dust. Under the bags lay a folded piece of white paper, which Maud unfolded and read. Satisfied with what she had previously written, she refolded the paper and replaced it under the little bags.

She closed the book and laid it beside her on the bed. Hesitating a moment, she lifted the lid of the bedside box and felt around under a bundle of clothes for her Aunt Jane's silver hand mirror. Her hands shook as she gently pulled it from its gray flannel pouch.

Holding the lit candle close to her face, she slowly raised the mirror until she saw her reflection. She gasped and let the mirror fall to her lap. Then, she slowly raised it again, and held it before her face. A large tear welled up. The image swam and broadened as though mocking her passionate wish to be accepted by her people. Maud squeezed her eye shut, and the tear rolled down her cheek.

"I can't, I can't," Maud whispered. "Oh, Emile, how I wish I could. How I wish to be with those who would love me, and look upon me as you once did. I've been locked away behind this ugly face for so long. How I wish to end my lonely exile."

She sighed heavily and wiped the tear from her face. Earlier, Big John and Johnny had made her sense of loneliness seem less intense. *They are my blood, after all*, she thought. Who better to entrust her innermost emotions, her past history, and her last wishes for her eventual passing? She felt comforted by their love and concern.

She lit the kerosene lantern with the candle, carefully returned the mirror to its flannel pouch, and opened the door to the little courtyard. The sky was still light, but it had clouded over, and the smell of rain was in the air. Behind the well, in a corner of her mostly dormant garden, little green shoots were beginning to appear from remnants of onions left in the ground. To the left of the garden plot, a large round rock stood against the canyon wall. It marked the entrance to her root cellar. Maud walked across the courtyard, put down the lantern, and rolled the rock about three feet from where it had stood. She brushed away some vines and small stones and found the iron ring attached to a heavy oak door stained with pitch.

Gathering the lantern and the mirror in one hand, she stepped down onto the rungs of a heavy ladder and descended into the darkness until she reached the dirt floor. Holding the light aloft, she walked a few feet into a chamber eight feet in diameter with a tunnel leading into the mine on the opposite wall. Around the walls stood a shovel, pickax, and several pans of different sizes for washing and separating gold from its gravel. There were also two or three small rusty ore-car wheels and an assortment of chisels, hammers, and gardening tools.

From a deep stone ledge above this cache, and behind dozens of jars of preserved food, Maud pulled out a small, half-filled burlap sack and let it fall to the ground. She untied the knot at the top and randomly withdrew a small ore sample. A gold nugget, half the size of a pea, gleamed dully in the lamplight. She put the nugget in the pocket of her skirt. Having no desire to see her image again in her lifetime, she placed the mirror inside the sack, secured it, and returned it to its hiding place.

As she turned back to the ladder, she thought she heard a sound. She stopped and cocked her head toward the open tunnel. She heard it again—a high-pitched, drawn-out echo, barely audible, coming from somewhere in the mine. She quickly blew out the lantern, and slowed her breathing to listen. At first it sounded like a baby's cry. As she listened, the sound became fainter until it trailed off to silence.

Bewildered and vaguely uneasy, but needing to return to her cabin for the purpose she had in mind, Maud felt her way along the wall in the darkness to the ladder. Back in her little cabin, with paper and pencil before her on the table, she prepared to write a letter to Big John. She withdrew the nugget from her pocket and placed it next to the paper. She began to write, but the sounds she had heard beyond the root cellar had piqued her curiosity and prevented her from concentrating. She relit the lantern and went back down into the root cellar. She entered the adjoining tunnel and stopped to listen. Nothing. She continued to walk, stopping to listen every few feet. At the intersection of a larger tunnel, Maud discovered two sets of fresh boot prints.

Seventeen

Before sundown, the two search groups had made a complete circle of the area and had met up at Ralph Larson's place. Jack Tatum and his men had searched about seven square miles of the woods to the east and north of the mine. Graywolf and his crew had covered a slightly greater area on their way south and west from Windsor Junction.

The weather had changed halfway through the search, and dark clouds were moving in from the coast. The men who followed Jack Tatum gathered behind Larson's barn with Jimmy Callahan and his hounds. They had not picked up a scent around the lake, in the woods, or along the railroad tracks. Jimmy threw down Luke's shirt that he'd used for scenting the dogs, unleashed them, and slumped into an old tractor seat to roll a cigarette. A couple of lumbermen brought out flasks of whiskey and passed them around while they waited for Tom Graywolf and the other half of his gang to come out of the woods. The men finally emerged on the west side. They looked exhausted and discouraged, and it was obvious that they had had no luck. Two of the tracking dogs paid no attention. They bounded playfully around the open field. But one of them, running at top speed in Graywolf's direction, suddenly veered off to the right toward the mine. At the outcropping, it ran back and forth, baying and sniffing at the foot of the rocks, pawing and jumping for a foothold. Was this the path that Luke and Charlie had taken? Excited by their barking companion, the other two dogs raced to the outcropping, frantically baying and scratching at the big boulders.

Hearing the dogs' commotion, Jimmy Callahan threw down his cigarette and jumped up. "They found a scent!" he yelled. "Come on, boys. The dogs found a scent!"

Graywolf saw Jimmy take off across the field with a dozen men following on his heels, including Graywolf's four other sons. Billy Lightfoot, arriving just at that moment, leaped from his horse and ran with Jimmy and the others. Graywolf and his men broke from the edge of the woods at a run, catching up with the others at the outcropping.

"They're in the mine!" yelled Jimmy Callahan to Graywolf. "The dogs got the scent!"

Graywolf ordered his men to hold off, but a few ignored him and started climbing the rocks, urged on by the cheering and yelling of the others.

"What're we waitin' for? We're goin' in!" shouted one of Graywolf's men.

"Let's go, let's go!" they roared.

"There's a path up here!" Jean-Paul Laval, the big, bearded lumber truck driver, called from the top of the rocks. "All right, you men. Let's find the old hag and get them boys back!"

"Yeah!" the men shouted in unison, brandishing rocks and clenched fists.

"We knew it! We guessed they was in the mine right from the start!" two farmers called to Jack Tatum.

Watching Tom Graywolf scream orders, his neck veins distended, Jack cocked his rifle and fired a shot into the air.

The men fell silent. Those on the rocks looked down to see who had fired a gun.

"Ain't nobody goin' into the mine tonight," Jack Tatum yelled in an angry voice. "It'll be dark in an hour, and a storm is comin.' It's dangerous up there even in daylight. Your men don't know the mine, Tom. They ain't from around here. They don't know the lay of the land, let alone where the cave-ins might be."

"Don't you want your boy back, mister?" called another man from the rocks. "We ain't afraid of the old crone."

"Old Maud ain't none of your business," Jack replied. "If the boys are lost in the mine, we'll find 'em—me and my neighbors. Your job is done here. You helped us find a trail, and we thank you. Now, you men come on down from them rocks, and Graywolf here will take you back to camp. Your truck is parked back of the barn."

"Now just a minute here, Jack," sputtered Graywolf. "My boy might be in there, too. If I want my men to start lookin' before *or* after dark, they'll start lookin'," he said, hoping to save face in front of his sons, although common sense told him that Jack Tatum was right.

"Well, then, you go right ahead, Tom. But you'll be responsible if they don't come back out." Jack turned to his neighbors. "If any of you men want to follow Tom Graywolf into the mine tonight, mark my words, you'll go at your own risk."

The farmers shuffled and murmured among themselves, then turned to go.

"I'll need your help again tomorrow, men. Can I count on you to be at Herb's gatehouse at sunup?"

"You can count on me, Jack," said Jimmy Callahan. "I'll bring the dogs."

Before they left, Max, Cyril, Ralph Larson, Billy Lightfoot, and all the other men volunteered to come back early the next morning.

Jack put a hand on Graywolf's arm. "I'm tellin' you like you told me and Elma. No use worryin'. I have a feelin' the boys are all right. It'll be sunup before you know it. If they're in the mine, we'll find 'em. I can deal with anything except the notion that Charlie was unhappy at home. I'm thankful my boy ain't runnin' away."

Graywolf looked into Jack's eyes, turned his back, and walked away.

At the lumber camp later that evening, Jean-Paul Laval took charge—with the help of the liquor he had stashed in his duffel bag.

"Drink up, men," he urged as he slopped whiskey in each man's cup. "Today was a hard day, a long day, and nothin' to show for it," he said with a sneer. "Have a drink, Graywolf," he shouted as Graywolf entered the bunkhouse. "It's a nasty night, and tomorrow's a workin' day. Nothin' can be done about your lost boy tonight, so have a drink and drown your sorrow."

"Graywolf is *grandmere*," snorted one of the crew, his French mixed with English. "Old ladies don't drink with the boys."

"Graywolf don't drink. Graywolf don't do nothin'. What kind of papa is Graywolf?" squealed another.

"We know who took them boys," hooted Jean-Paul, pouring another drink. "The witch got 'em. We can find 'em. Why wait 'til mornin'?"

"Yeah," they all shouted drunkenly.

"Now listen to me, men," shouted Graywolf. "I'm the boss here. You do as I say. Leave Old Maud out of this. You're barkin' up the wrong tree," he said, remembering Jake's words.

His friend was right. This thing had gone too far. His worry over Luke had weakened his control over the men; he hadn't tried to stop their drinking. Luke was lost out there somewhere, and it was all his fault. He wanted to cry, but he knew that the men would destroy him if he showed any further weakness.

Graywolf straightened his shoulders. "The mine is danger-ous. My boy is all right. He ain't no dummy; he's a brave boy. He can take care of himself. We'll all go at daybreak and fetch him from the mine and—"

Jean-Paul, who had sneaked up behind Graywolf, struck him on the back of the head with an empty whiskey bottle. Graywolf fell forward, sprawling unconscious on the bunkhouse floor.

"Ah, our fearless Graywolf," sneered Jean-Paul. "Leader of the pack. Look at him, boys—more like a mama bear cryin' for her cub."

The men laughed and passed the whiskey. Jean-Paul ordered the men to tie Graywolf to the foot of one of the bunks.

"I say tomorrow may be too late," snapped Jean-Paul. "Who knows what this witch has in mind for those boys? I say we go into the mine tonight!"

"Yeah!" shouted the men. "We go tonight. Through the storm, when the witch is in the lair. Kill the witch and bring the boys home safe. Yeah!"

Lightning flashed through the cracks of the camp shutters, and rain lashed the tin roof. As thunder rumbled overhead, fifteen men armed with lanterns, ax handles, peaveys, and whiskey bottles staggered from Graywolf's camp, scrambled onto the flatbed truck, and headed for the mine gate.

Eighteen

"They're a rough bunch," Billy reported to Big John and Nathan when he reached home. "The makings of a lynch mob, if you ask me. It's going to take more than the four of us to hold Herb Norris's gate if Graywolf's boys try to break through."

Billy continued to fill them in. "Herb radioed his main office about what's going on, but he doesn't expect any help from them. They advised him to contact the local authorities. I warned Sheriff Cabot on my way home from Herb's. He told me that he and Claude are the only officers assigned to Beaver Creek. He said it would take almost two days to get more men here to help. The sheriff thinks the storm will keep Graywolf's men in camp. He just doesn't seem to understand the seriousness of what could happen here tonight. I asked him to check on the mine gate anyway. He agreed to do what he could."

Billy poured himself a cup of coffee from the pot on the back of the stove. "When I left the sheriff's office, I doubled back to Callahan's place and told them we needed help. Jack Tatum and Milligan were there. They're rounding up the others to meet at Herb's at eight o'clock tonight."

Big John looked at the mantel clock. It was six forty-five. He rose from the head of the table and issued orders to his sons. "Nathan, break out the guns and ammunition. Billy, you ride Ruby down to Cobequid Road at the rail crossing and wait behind the Big Rock. Watch the road at Dixon's hill and fire a shot to let us know when Graywolf and his men are on their way. Make sure you get to Herb's before they do. We'll need all hands at the gate."

More orders followed in quick succession. "Nathan, get what railroad flares we have from the barn and wrap them in a tarp. Load them onto the truck along with the lanterns and some extra kerosene. We need to light up the gate to keep those men from climbing over the fence in the dark. We've got to keep them in sight at all times."

During these past few days, Big John seemed suddenly younger and stronger than Johnny ever remembered. This must be what his grandfather had been like when he was younger: a man to be reckoned with. Johnny felt proud. He sat beside his father at the table, and waited for Big John's orders for *his* part in the night's work. He could feel the tension and excitement building. Since his thirteenth birthday, hadn't the Lightfoot men included him in all important family decisions? He was now almost thirteen and a half, even more of a man. He waited for his orders.

From talk that Johnny had overheard when Mr. Milligan rode to his farm with Mr. Norris's alarm, the men of Beaver Creek had committed themselves to protecting Maud against Graywolf's ruffians. They had given her the benefit of the doubt with respect to the disappearance of the two boys. Innocent until proven guilty, they said. Johnny wanted to be a part of what he knew to be true.

Glancing from one face to another, Johnny waited. Big John recognized his grandson's expression—intense, eager, and excited– and it was difficult for him to say, "Whether you come with us or not is up to your father, Johnny. You understand?"

Johnny swallowed hard, a seed of disappointment suddenly taking root. "Yes, Grandfather. I understand." He turned to his father.

"Johnny," Nathan began hesitantly. "I know how much you want to be a part of this. Your grandfather, Billy, and I . . . well, we've never before had to face such dangerous men. We don't know what to expect. They're tough, drunk, and unreasonable. They're not really interested in finding Luke and Charlie. They're on a witch hunt. They're a mob now. There might be shooting. If anything were to happen to you, I'd never forgive myself, and neither would your mother. I'm asking you to stay behind and keep watch here."

Nathan looked imploringly at his wife. Mary felt sad at seeing her son's utter dismay, yet relieved about Nathan's decision to keep him out of harm's way.

"But Maud has to be warned, Father! Who's going to warn Maud?" demanded Johnny, tears of profound disappointment filling his eyes.

"I have a feeling that Maud already knows about this. She'll know what to do. She knows the mine better than anybody in Beaver Creek. Besides, Graywolf's men won't get through the gate. I promise you that. Besides protecting Maud, it's Herb's responsibility to keep those men out of the mine for their own safety. Will you stay, Johnny, and keep Chum here with you?"

Disappointment turned to resentment as Johnny resigned himself to his father's request. A muscle twitched in his jaw. "I guess I don't have a choice, do I?"

"I'm sorry, Son. You don't."

Big John took a shotgun from his bedroom and placed it, with extra shells, near the door. Nathan checked Johnny's .22 and made sure there was plenty of ammunition. He hoped that Johnny wouldn't need to use either weapon.

"Please be careful, Nathan," said Mary, her arms encircling her husband.

"I don't know what time we'll be back. Keep only the kitchen lamp lit, and don't open the door for anyone," said Nathan, casting a sympathetic glance at Johnny as he followed Big John and Billy out the door. The wind had picked up, and it had already begun to rain.

Nineteen

Luke and Charlie finished sharing a candy bar and a raw carrot. Luke saved another candy bar and two hard-boiled eggs in his saddlebag. They sipped water from an old army flask with an attached screw top.

They agreed to make one more attempt to find the shaft entrance before the batteries in the flashlight gave out for good. Luke explained to Charlie that when people are lost, they generally walk in a circle. Luke thought they should make absolutely no turns off one chosen main tunnel, but follow it as straight as possible. That way, he said, they were bound to surface somewhere in the open mine, or maybe over on the other side of Cobequid Road.

Charlie thought it would be a good idea to call out for help in case Mr. Norris, even a trespasser, might be somewhere nearby. Luke agreed that it couldn't hurt.

Charlie gave the signal. "We'll count to three, then holler 'help' as loud as we can. Okay?"

"Okay," said Luke, clearing his throat in preparation.

"One, two, three. HELP! HELP! HELP!" they screamed until they were flushed and hoarse.

Their voices echoed over and over through the shafts and caverns of the mine. They listened to their cries bouncing off the walls of a labyrinth of tunnels until the words became distorted—sounding almost inhuman. The sound frightened them and reminded them just how vast the mine really was.

Charlie was spooked and grabbed Luke's arm.

What worried Luke most were the big puddles of water they were forced to cross trying to keep on a straight path. He had the feeling that they were still walking slightly downhill, which they earlier recognized as a mistake and had turned around. The musty smell of earth and rotting wood was stronger than ever, and the cold dampness was bone chilling.

The boys continued on this "straight-as-possible" path until the water was almost to their knees. Still, they were determined to keep on, desperately hoping that the straight tunnel would eventually carry them uphill again and into the open.

"I don't mind tellin' you, I'm really scared. The water is seepin' through the cracks in the walls. God knows how long we been down here. It might even be Sunday. Do you s'pose they're lookin' for us? I know my folks must be worried sick about me. I'm awful tired and hungry and scared. Tell me straight, Luke, man-to-man. Are we gonna die down here?"

"No, Charlie, no. Now listen. There's a way out and we're gonna find it. Besides, your pa and old Herb Norris are prob'ly lookin' for us right now."

By the dim light of the flashlight, Luke and Charlie continued through the dark water. But then, directly ahead, they saw a jumbled wreck of charred timbers, debris, and rock barring their path. Water trickled down over the rocks and between the charred boards and blackened barrels.

"Good god!" said Charlie. "It looks like a house fell into this tunnel. How're we gonna get around that?"

"We're not," Luke said flatly. "I've got a bad feelin' about this place, Charlie. We got to go back."

The boys ran back through the water the way they had come. When they reached what seemed to be the crest of a hill and drier ground, they stopped to rest, listening to the dripping water. They watched helplessly as the weak light grew dimmer, until it finally gave out completely. Luke frantically shook the flashlight as if trying to extract a few more minutes of light. Charlie gasped and backed up against Luke. Sudden and total darkness left them no further choices. Luke squeezed his eyes closed a few seconds, then opened them wide. Had there been any daylight coming from anywhere, he would have been able to see a soft glow. But he saw nothing but blackness.

Charlie clutched at Luke and sobbed. "Please hang on to me, Luke. Don't let go."

Twenty

From a darkened window of the Lightfoot house, Johnny watched Big John's truck cross the track and head up Cobequid Road. He pulled the shades on the downstairs windows, and blew out all the lamps except the one in the kitchen. He made sure that the locks on the front and kitchen doors were secured, and checked to see that both guns were loaded. Upstairs he settled the little ones and made them promise to be quiet. His ten-year-old brother, Seth, assured Johnny that he was ready to help, and that he could fire a gun.

"Don't you worry, Seth. We're safe here. Just keep the babies quiet, and don't let them get out of bed," said Johnny, tousling Seth's hair.

Back in the kitchen, Johnny anxiously paced and watched the clock. From his place by the hearth, Chum followed Johnny's movements with his eyes, his big head resting on his front paws. The storm was worsening. The wind whistled around the corners of the house and honked at the upstairs windows.

At nine-fifteen Johnny heard a distant shot. It was Billy's signal. Graywolf and his men were on their way.

Johnny turned down the flame in the kitchen lamp and

raised the window shade an inch from the sill. The bright lights of a truck had already reached the bottom of Dixon's hill. He watched as the headlights pierced the heavy rain, followed Cobequid Road past Bottomless Pond, and crossed the tracks. Johnny shoved his sweaty hands deep into his pockets.

Seated at the kitchen table, Mary watched Johnny's agitation. The shot startled her even though she had expected it and knew what it meant. For an hour she had struggled with the decision to send Johnny into the mine to warn Maud. She opened the kitchen door to the back porch, found Johnny's oil slicker, and stood before him, holding it open.

Johnny searched his mother's face. "What are you doing?" he asked.

"Johnny, I would go with you if I could. My fear for Maud's safety is as great as your own. You must hurry. Graywolf's men will soon be at the gate."

"But you heard me give Father my word—"

"If he returns before you do, I'll tell him I encouraged you to go. Those men are bent on finding Maud. If they do, they'll kill her, Johnny. Bring her here where she'll be safe. You must take your path to the second level of the mine. Chum will help you find the way. No harm will come to you; I know that the Great Spirit will protect you. Hurry now. I have a lantern ready." She held out her hand. "And here are some extra shells for your .22."

Johnny felt an overwhelming pride and respect for his mother as she kissed his forehead and held him tightly. Then he and Chum departed into the stormy night. They crossed the tracks and hurried on to the big rock. From the light of the lantern, Johnny recognized Ruby's hoof prints. They were filled with rainwater, but the mare's droppings were still intact.

Patches of snow left on the ground hid Johnny's old trail marks, and when he reached the familiar burned-out stump, the trees and bushes tossed so wildly in the gusting wind that they obscured the path he was looking for. But Chum found it. A few feet ahead, he stood at the base of the trees, barking for Johnny to follow. Heavy rain pelted them from behind as they scrambled up the incline. Struggling on all fours, Johnny slipped back a few times on the patchy snow and wet rocks, but Chum dug his feet into the shale, and his sturdy legs carried him quickly to the top.

"Hold on, Chum," Johnny yelled into the wind. "Don't get too far ahead. Wait up, boy."

At last Johnny reached the second level. Leaning into the wind, he looked back down over Cobequid Road and across the orchard to his darkened house. Farther up the road, lamplight flickered in a few windows to guide loved ones home. The lightning flashed through the eastern sky, reflecting off the watery surface of Cobequid Road like a silver snake. Thunder exploded and rolled over the hills. At this height above the valley, there was no shelter from the strong gusts and heavy rain that blew in from the ocean in dense, horizontal sheets.

"Stay close, boy," Johnny shouted. He took Chum's face between his hands and looked into the dog's blinking eyes. "Help me find the way to Maud. We've got to find Maud. Good dog."

The thunder crashed, and the wind howled unchecked over the flat desolation of the mine. With each flash of lightning the path became visible, but only a few feet ahead. The wet boulders seemed to move with every streak of light from the sky, threatening to trip Johnny and bar his way. In the halo of light from the lantern, sinister black shadows behind big rocks undulated and grew. The strong wind blew the rain from all directions— now at his back, pushing him forward, then in his face, stinging his eyes as he struggled to keep Chum in sight. Johnny was sure that the spirits were testing his strength and courage. He set his jaw, straightened his back, and forged ahead toward Maud's cabin.

Against the angry elements, Johnny would call to Chum, and the dog would bark and run back to let Johnny know where he was on the path. They came to the vertical shaft where Johnny had fallen through. The water had eroded the rim of the shaft where Herb's new planks once rested. Its widened mouth gaped black and ominous a few feet ahead. The wind swept over the opening, screaming eerily into its depths like tortured ghosts. Fearing the strength of the gusts, Johnny crawled on hands and knees past the opening, his heart pounding. Chum crouched close to Johnny and crawled between him and the edge of the hole. Bracing himself against the wind, ears pinned back, Chum whined and barked until they were out of danger.

When they finally reached the entrance to Maud's canyon between the high walls, the roaring wind was high overhead, its voice tamed to a deep moan. Johnny breathed a sigh of relief.

The path to Maud's cabin seemed longer than he remembered, and farther into the canyon. Chum suddenly ran ahead up the path, then returned barking, his tail wagging.

A few more feet and Johnny's light reflected in Maud's window. All was in darkness. As he tread upon the first step, Maud flung open the door, and he gasped to see a double-barreled shotgun pointed between his eyes.

"Maud, it's me, Johnny," he called in a high whisper. "It's Johnny Lightfoot and Chum."

Chum whined. Johnny held the lantern up to his wet face.

"Johnny! What are you doing here? Quick, come inside," said Maud.

"I came to tell you that Charlie Tatum and Luke Graywolf are lost, maybe somewhere in the mine," Johnny said breathlessly. There was no time for details. "Graywolf's men are on their way into the mine to look for them. They're looking for you, too, Maud. They think you're responsible for Charlie and Luke's disappearance. They're a rough bunch—drinking and out of control. I came to warn you and take you to our house, where you'll be safe."

"I know about Graywolf's men. I saw them on the rocks today near Larson's farm. When I saw your light, I was afraid it was them. They'll come through Herb's gate, where they think it's safe, but never mind that now. I know where the boys are. I tracked them through the mine earlier today. I probably could have located them then, but I hadn't prepared, and my lamp oil was low. They are very deep in the mine. I've just returned for more kerosene and lanterns. I'm going back down."

"Then I'm going with you."

"No, Johnny. You can't go with me this time. The timbers are giving out, rotted through. Water is seeping in from everywhere. I've never seen it like this. I know I can find the boys. I know where they are. Stay here and wait for me, but I must go right now."

Johnny put his hand on Maud's arm and looked directly into her eye.

"Maud, I can't let you go alone. Grandfather would be ashamed of me if he knew. We are blood kin, and I must protect you and help you as I would my family at home. My father says I'm a man now. Please, don't let me disappoint him."

Maud's face softened. "All right, Johnny. Come, we must hurry. I will show you a secret way."

Maud handed him two lanterns and a can of kerosene as they slipped out the back door of the cabin. Maud's black cape flapped around her shoulders like giant bat wings as she led the way past the well to the trapdoor. Halfway down the ladder, Johnny reached up and carried Chum down to the dirt floor. In the light, he was surprised to see the size and the contents of the underground room.

"My root cellar," explained Maud. She unfastened her cape and let it fall to the ground. As she hurried through to the adjoining tunnel, she snapped, "Come, quick. We have a distance to go before we reach the boys."

Twenty-one

Billy Lightfoot had raced his mare up Cobequid Road as soon as he saw the lights of Graywolf's flatbed truck at the top of Dixon's hill. He had fired the warning shot, then headed toward Mine Hill at a gallop. He dismounted quickly at Herb's gatehouse, where some of the Lightfoots' neighbors were milling about at the bottom of the road. Herb's pickup was parked broadside against the gate between deep ditches on either side. Some of the men, having heard Billy's shot, stood in the back of the truck with guns loaded. Lanterns hung from the gate and the truck. Nathan Lightfoot and Graywolf's four sons stood nearby with flares.

After a few minutes, the flatbed truck pulled up a few feet onto Mine Hill and stopped. The bright headlights illuminated Herb's pickup, with the men standing ready in back. Herb stepped out of the shadows and walked slowly toward the flatbed truck and its driver. Jean-Paul Laval stuck an arm out the window, signaling his men to stay where they were. He seemed less confident when he saw the number of men at the gate.

"Whatever you boys have in mind, you can hold it right there," shouted Herb over the wind.

"And who might you be, and what business do you have here?" demanded Jean-Paul.

"I'm Herb Norris, government official and gatekeeper of Beaver Creek Mine. Who are you, and where is Graywolf?"

"Graywolf is sleepin' off his whiskey in camp," he said with a laugh. "He sent me, Jean-Paul Laval, and these men to help find the boys in the mine. Where we find the witch, we find the boys."

"Well, Jean-Paul, you just turn this truck around and go back the way you came. Nobody's going into the mine tonight or any other night. The mine is officially closed—has been for years."

"We take orders from Graywolf, and Graywolf says we help find the boys. Today we found nothin'. Tonight we'll have better luck," said Jean-Paul, getting down from behind the wheel and beckoning to his men.

Jack Tatum jumped down from Herb's pickup, followed by five other men, including Billy Lightfoot and Ralph Larson, gun barrels glistening in the rain.

"You're lyin', Laval," Jack yelled. "Graywolf don't drink. He didn't send you up here tonight. Anyway, we don't need or want your help to find our boys. This is none of your business. You heard what Herb said. Take your men and clear out."

All of Jean-Paul's men alighted from the truck and stood beside him, waving their ax handles and peaveys menacingly. The two groups of men stood glaring at each other, braced for a fight. Several of Jean-Paul's men walked around to the back of the truck, talking among themselves. The Callahan brothers and Nathan Lightfoot, fearing a plot to rush and climb the fence, lighted two flares and placed them at its base. Jean-Paul smiled crookedly, seeming to wonder if these simple farmers, brandishing their guns, would actually shoot a man. As though reading Jean-Paul's mind, Big John stepped to within a few feet of him and slowly raised the barrel of his rifle level with Jean-Paul's eyes. Then he drew back the bolt and, with a loud clatter, drove a cartridge into the chamber.

At that moment, a white station wagon with the sheriff's emblem pulled up beside the flatbed truck. Sheriff Cabot and his deputy, Claude, in bright yellow slickers, came around the truck. Immediately sizing up the situation, the sheriff strode up to Big John.

"Looks like we're just in time, Big John." He laid his hand on the barrel of Big John's rifle, forcing the muzzle to the ground. Turning to Jean-Paul, he asked, "Where's Graywolf?"

"Graywolf's not here. He's like a drunken old lady. I'm Jean-Paul Laval. Graywolf put me in charge tonight."

"In charge of what, Laval?" asked Sheriff Cabot, looking into Jean-Paul's shifty eyes.

"I'm in charge of these men who come to find Graywolf's son," Jean-Paul sneered, straightening himself.

"And what do you think you can do up there in the dark in this storm?" asked Cabot. He didn't wait for an answer. "I'll tell you what you'll do. You'll either drown in a sinkhole, fall into a bottomless shaft, or get buried alive in a cave-in."

Sheriff Cabot smiled into Jean-Paul's face. "See, Graywolf's no dummy," he said with a wink and a nod. "He knows about the cave-ins and mudslides. Do you think he'd risk his neck up there? No, he sends fools like you to do his dirty work."

"It's not Graywolf's idea. It's mine," blurted Jean-Paul, flustered and confused, his resolve fading even as his cronies itched for a fight.

"Then you're even more stupid than I thought." Sheriff Cabot looked away in disgust.

The muscles twitched in Jean-Paul's jaw. Determined to save face in front of the other lumbermen, he summoned a weasel-faced lumberjack from behind the truck. The man whispered something into his ear. Jean-Paul nodded slightly and smiled. Weasel Face went back to his place behind the truck with the others. A moment later, three men suddenly rushed toward Big John, Jack, and Herb, knocking Jack to the ground. During the scuffle that followed, Weasel Face slipped unnoticed from behind the truck, dropped into the deep ditch on the right side of the road, and stealthily made his way between the fence and the unlit side of Herb's pickup. He slowly opened the door, slid inside, and waited for the signal to release the hand brake.

Meanwhile, Sheriff Cabot drew his pistol and fired a shot into the air. Jean-Paul's men disengaged themselves from the struggle. Cursing and swearing, they walked slowly back to the truck.

Approaching the sheriff with an affable smile, Jean-Paul raised his hands in submission. "All right, Sheriff. Since our help ain't wanted here, we'll head back to camp."

Jean-Paul turned to his men. "Okay, boys," he shouted, "back on the truck. We're goin' back to camp and wait for daylight."

Without protest, the lumbermen climbed onto the truck. Laughing, Jean-Paul swung himself up into the cab and started the motor. He backed the truck slowly out onto Cobequid Road, sounded the horn twice, and disappeared.

"They gave up too easy," said Jack Tatum, wiping mud from his face. "I don't trust that Jean-Paul fella. I think they're up to somethin'."

The other men agreed and hunched uneasily inside their slickers.

"Naw, they won't be back," said Sheriff Cabot. "It's mighty nasty out here. They'll go back to camp and sleep it off, like Graywolf."

"Jean-Paul lied," said Big John. "Graywolf doesn't drink."

"Well, we can't worry about Graywolf just now," said Jack Tatum. "He can take care of himself. We're stickin' around here 'til daybreak. We'll be goin' into the mine to find the boys as soon as it's light enough. How about you, Sheriff?"

"Sorry, Jack. We've got other business in the county. I'm confident you'll find your boys with all the help you have here." Cabot gestured toward the farmers standing around in the rain. "We're spread out kinda thin, me and Claude here. Tell you what I'll do, though. On the way out to the highway, we'll stop by Graywolf's camp to check on him and see if those fellas are behaving themselves."

The men walked behind the sheriff's car to the end of Mine Hill and watched as his headlights moved along Cobequid Road and disappeared. As they walked back up Mine Hill toward the gate, they heard Herb's pickup sound its horn and saw it roll slowly and quietly down the incline toward the deep ditch to the left of the gate. As they watched helplessly, the pickup's front end dipped and settled into the rushing water of the gully. At the same time, Jean-Paul's lumber truck, lights off and horn blaring, came roaring at full speed up Mine Hill, the men in back laughing and throwing whiskey bottles. Horror stricken, Jack Tatum yelled, "Look out!" His men scattered, diving into the brush at the side of the road.

Laughing like a madman, Jean-Paul held the accelerator to the floor. The tires spun into the roadbed, spitting mud and gravel into the air. The truck crashed through the gate, sending posts and barbed wire flying into the woods and onto the roof of Herb's gatehouse. The men on the back held on, some laughing drunkenly and others yelling desperately. Just beyond the gate, Jean-Paul downshifted, jammed the gearshift into second, and slowed just enough to let Weasel Face jump on the running board. Jean-Paul again shifted gears and sped up the hill toward the clearing, while Jack Tatum, the Lightfoots, and the other men ran for Big John's truck, parked behind the gatehouse.

Sheriff Cabot and Claude pulled into Graywolf's camp. The sawmill was dark, but a light shone from Graywolf's office window at the other end of the building. They walked up the steps and tried the office door. It was locked. Cabot looked through the window, but he couldn't see anything out of place.

Claude looked around the yard. "Hey, Sheriff. Those boys oughta been back from Herb's by now, but the truck ain't here, and Graywolf's pickup is parked over by the bunkhouse."

"They probably went into town to raise more hell," said the sheriff. "Better check the pickup and the bunkhouse."

They crossed the muddy yard and pulled open the door of Graywolf's truck. It was empty. Claude motioned toward the bunkhouse, the lights showing through the slats of the window shutters. Peering through the cracks, Claude saw men sprawled drunkenly on several of the bunks. At the foot of one bunk was another man, gagged and sitting upright on the floor with his back to the windows, struggling to free his wrists, which were tied behind him with rope. He was bleeding from a head wound.

"Holy mackerel, Sheriff! Looka here!"

Sheriff Cabot was at the window in three long strides.

"Good god, it's Graywolf. He's hurt!" exclaimed the sheriff.

They rushed around to the bunkhouse door, but found it locked. Claude looked questioningly at Sheriff Cabot, who nodded his approval. They backed up a few feet and lowered their husky shoulders together. Then charging forward, they shattered the door from its frame. Graywolf looked startled, obviously expecting to see Jean-Paul and his hoodlums. Relief lit up his bloodshot eyes when he recognized the sheriff. Claude removed Graywolf's gag and gave him some water, then freed his hands and feet, helped him stand, and led him to a cot.

"Who did this to you, Graywolf?" Sheriff Cabot asked, examining his wound.

"It was Jean-Paul . . . Jean-Paul Laval. He's a crazy man—always was a troublemaker. Shoulda fired him months ago. Got the boys riled up. To be honest, Sheriff, I . . . I brought *this* trouble on myself. It's all my fault. I thought my Luke was runnin' away from home. I couldn't blame him if he was." Graywolf's eyes filled with tears, but he quickly recovered.

"I haven't been a good father to my kids, especially Luke. He needs attention, needs love. I failed him bad. Now it's too late. I hired this scum to find my boy, bring him home. I shoulda known they'd get out of hand, drinkin' and all. And I was wrong about Old Maud. We all were. I got to find my boy and save Old Maud from that mob."

Graywolf jumped to his feet and swayed. The sheriff eased him back onto the cot.

"Take it easy, Graywolf. That's a nasty cut," he cautioned, applying a bandage from the bunkhouse first-aid box.

"Call Sheriff Buck, in Wellington," Cabot said to Claude. "Tell him we have an emergency right here in our own backyard. Tell him I'm sending you on ahead. I'll be there as soon as I can clear up matters here. I'm taking Graywolf to Dr. LeBrun; then I'm going after Jean-Paul Laval and arresting him for assault and inciting a mob."

"I ain't goin' to no doctor until I find my boy," Graywolf told Cabot. "I'm goin' with the sheriff," he said to Claude, as if he wanted that message also relayed to Sheriff Buck, in Wellington.

After Claude drove off in the sheriff's car, Graywolf's pickup headed for Mine Hill with Sheriff Cabot behind the wheel and Graywolf by his side.

Twenty-two

Maud walked so fast that Johnny could hardly keep up. After a half hour, she slowed her pace and explained their position. "We are very close to where I found the boys' tracks. We have come well over a mile at this point. It has been a long time since I've been this deep in the mine—not since the tavern fire. Hopefully, the boys have not moved very far. They probably have no light by now. Soon we will come to a long ladder reaching up through an opening in the ceiling of a large tunnel. We will leave two lighted lanterns there to make sure we find it again. It's our escape ladder to the surface."

Within minutes they entered the high tunnel, whose floor pitched slightly downhill. Johnny found the ladder, the top of which disappeared into the gloom above. Reaching high above his head, he caught the first rung and climbed halfway up. He hooked two lanterns to the rungs, but the light barely penetrated the dark, cavernous space. He lifted his face to the rain and fresh air that rushed down through the opening. With two remaining lanterns, which they refilled from what was left in the kerosene can, they pushed on for another few minutes. The floor of the shaft became muddier where the powdery silt had absorbed water.

Maud suddenly stopped and raised her lamp. There in the mud were two sets of relatively fresh boot tracks. Picking up a scent, Chum pointed his nose into the drafty tunnel and began to bark.

"They're not far now," said Maud. "They should be able to hear the dog. Let Chum bark a moment, then we must listen."

Chum ran down the tunnel a short distance, barking loudly. Then Johnny called him back and closed his hands around the dog's muzzle. Maud and Johnny held their breath to listen in the semidarkness. They heard nothing. Johnny released Chum and let him run again, barking. When Johnny whistled, Chum returned the second time. Maud put a finger to her lips.

"Listen, Johnny," Maud whispered. "Do you hear that?"

Johnny turned and cupped his ear in the direction of the deep tunnel. "Yes. I *do* hear something. It sounds a little bit like . . . like a baby crying."

"The echo in the tunnels from the great pressure on the walls down here makes it sound like that. But what you're hearing is the boys calling out, Johnny. They're not far. We must hurry. If the water covers their tracks, Chum will show us the way."

Another hundred feet farther into the tunnel, Maud and Johnny were over their ankles in water. Chum splashed alongside Johnny, his nose in the air, barking when the boys' voices became louder.

Sloshing through the water, they rounded a bend. There, huddled together on a rock like cornered, frightened animals, sat Luke and Charlie.

Charlie shielded his eyes from the light and began to cry. Luke put an arm around Charlie's neck and squinted into the light.

"Who's there?" called Luke in a tenuous voice.

"It's Johnny Lightfoot, Luke. And Old Maud. She tracked you. Are you all right, Charlie? Can you boys walk?"

"You found us! See, Charlie, I knew someone would come!" Luke jumped down from the rock into the water. It was much deeper than he expected.

Johnny moved closer to the boys and held up his lantern. When Luke saw Maud's face, he recoiled and gasped. Charlie screamed and scrambled farther back on the rock against the wall.

"Don't be afraid," Johnny said, at once sensitive to the boys' reaction and to Maud's reluctance to come closer. "Maud won't hurt you. She's our friend. She found you. Please, Charlie, trust me. Come down from the rock," he coaxed. "There's no time to explain now. We've got to get out of here. The water's coming in fast."

Maud stood silently holding her light aloft. Johnny held out his hand. "Charlie, we've got to go, *now*! I'd hate to leave you here but, so help me, I will if I have to."

Charlie inched his way forward to the edge of the rock. With his eyes riveted on Maud's face, he slid into the water beside Luke.

"Okay, Johnny, lead the way," said Luke.

Johnny turned and followed Maud, then Charlie, Luke, and Chum followed behind them. Over his shoulder, Johnny warned, "We will do exactly as Maud says, and we'll stay close together. Right?"

"Yes, Johnny," said Luke.

"R-right," said Charlie. "Just get us outta here."

They retraced their steps quickly. Maud was alarmed at how fast the water was pouring from the timbers overhead and from the walls in little rivulets. The water was now almost up to their knees, and Johnny could hear Charlie breathing heavily, struggling to keep up. Johnny hurried to catch up to Maud.

"The water's getting deeper," he said. "Chum and the boys are having trouble keeping up. How much farther to the ladder?"

"We must reach the crest of the hill," said Maud. "We'll make better time when the water isn't so deep."

Johnny pulled Luke along beside him until he began to feel the uphill drag on his legs. They were gradually coming out of the water with every step. Maud looked back. "Let the boy Charlie catch up. I'll help him along." Maud prayed that the old timbers would hold the walls back a little while longer. "Make sure Luke doesn't founder. Keep hold of Chum's collar."

Maud slowed until Charlie caught up to her. He kept his eyes straight ahead and chugged past, fear pumping adrenaline through his plump body. He was determined to run until his heart exploded rather than let Maud touch him. He could hear Luke and

Johnny panting behind. Chum was now better able to leap through the water, and ran ahead.

They were more than halfway up the hill and almost out of the water when they heard a deep, muffled rumble like a distant earthquake. The walls of the tunnel shook, and small rocks and muddy water oozed from between the jolted timbers. The floor beneath them trembled, and a great gust of musty air swept over and beyond them through the tunnel.

Maud grabbed at Charlie and pushed him ahead of her. "Run to the light!" she shouted. Charlie was so frightened that he took off without question into the darkness toward where Maud had pointed. Johnny and Luke stopped and looked back down the tunnel. Maud reached out and caught Luke by the collar and pushed him in the direction Charlie had gone. Chum followed right behind.

"Run, Johnny!" urged Maud. "Run as fast as you can! To the ladder, to the light!"

"Maud, what is it? Oh god, what was that awful sound?"

"The sinkhole is giving way. Run!"

Johnny reached for Maud's hand, gripping it tight as they ran up the incline toward the ladder and the lanterns they had hung there. The water rushing through the tunnels created a strong draft, pushing them from behind. Maud's wispy white hair blew forward over her face, and her black skirts billowed out in front of her. The hollow sound of groaning timbers, collapsing tunnels, and rushing water reached them. Reality hit Johnny like a punch in the stomach: *all five of them might drown!* The tragic irony flashed through his mind as he ran: had he been saved from death in the shaft only to drown in the mine after all?

Johnny kept calling to Luke and Charlie while keeping an iron grip on Maud's hand. They ran, clutching their lanterns, until they saw the boys jumping like frantic rats to reach the bottom rung of the tall ladder, several feet off the ground.

Johnny reached the ladder and shouted, "Quick, Charlie. Don't stop for anything." Lacing the fingers of both hands together, he made a toehold boost for Charlie, and lifted him to the second rung of the ladder. Charlie scrambled farther up and grabbed one of the lanterns, then stopped, paralyzed. Staring down into the tunnel, he pointed at a wave of water rushing toward them. Luke, on the bottom rung, quickly climbed to the next and turned to offer his hand to Maud. She handed him her lantern. Chum was suddenly struck broadside by the wave. It carried him, thrashing, past the ladder. Maud allowed the water to buoy her up enough to catch hold of the first rung. Then she quickly reached out and caught Chum's collar, pulled him back to the ladder, and pushed him, coughing and snorting, up behind Luke. While Maud and Johnny clung to the bottom of the ladder, Luke pushed Charlie's backside from below, yelling at him to keep moving.

The debris-filled water rose, clawing at Johnny and Maud as they started to climb. Johnny's lantern sputtered and went out. He let go of the handle, and the lantern swept past in the rushing water. "Keep going, Johnny!" Maud shouted, pushing him up the ladder ahead of her. "I'm right behind you."

Charlie, Luke, and Chum climbed through the ceiling opening to firm ground above at the edge of a thicket. Chum coughed and barked and looked down into the hole. Dropping to their bellies, Charlie and Luke dangled their lanterns into the cavern and yelled to Johnny, who grabbed the last lantern they had left hanging on the ladder and shone it down on Maud. The water was up to her shoulders. The strong current and floating debris tugged at her clothing as she tried to climb. Johnny backed down the ladder and reached for Maud's hand. She looked up, shook her head no, and shouted for him to keep moving. She climbed a few feet higher. Johnny watched to make sure that she was clear of the water before scrambling up toward the boys.

Another terrifying rumble shook the mine. A wall of black water suddenly exploded through the tall tunnel. It carried shattered timbers, which rammed the crumbling walls of the tunnel with crushing force and a deafening roar. One of the timbers struck the ladder, tearing away its bottom half. Luke and Charlie screamed from above. Johnny turned back, and froze. He saw Maud lose her footing and slip back into the water. The raging current pushed at her body as she clung with one hand to the remains of the ladder.

"Maud! Maud!" Johnny screamed. "Hang on, Maud!" He

slid back down. In the light from his lantern, he saw her grimace as she tried to turn her body against the current. Maud's skirts billowed on the roiling surface and floated around her face. Johnny's fingertips touched her hand. The grimace gone, she looked up into his eyes, her expression seemingly softened, even happy.

"My Bible, Johnny," she called up to him in a strong but strangely calm voice. "Keep my Bible." Johnny strained for a firm hold on Maud's hand as her fingers gradually loosened from the side of the ladder. As he watched in horror, her face disappeared beneath the surface of the water. In a second, she was swept away.

"Maud! Maud!" Johnny cried down into the raging water. He slid to the bottom rung. Holding the lantern above his head, he leaned over the water and screamed "Maud!" But she was gone. The water rose higher, and the current flowed stronger. He struggled to climb back up the ladder. Needing both hands, he had to let go of the lantern.

Johnny dragged himself up through the opening and stood looking down into the blackness below. "Maud," he whispered weakly.

The remains of the ladder broke away in the rushing water just below the opening. Johnny shuddered. He pulled Luke, Charlie, and Chum away from the hole and into the nearby thicket, fearing that the ground might cave in beneath their feet. He sat down heavily on a rock and covered his face with both hands. The rain and wind had stopped. A full moon and scudding clouds seemed to be racing in opposite directions through high, wispy fog. Except for the sound of moving water below, all was quiet and still.

Luke came and sat beside Johnny. "Old Maud saved our lives, Johnny. She gave her life to save us. I'm awful sorry. I'm so sorry." Luke's shoulders began to shake with sobs.

Johnny wiped a hand across his face. He put an arm around Luke's shoulders, sighed heavily, and stared wearily into the night.

"She was my kin," he said. "She was my blood kin. You didn't know that, did you?"

Luke and Charlie looked at Johnny in disbelief. "Really, Johnny?" asked Charlie, incredulously. "Is that the truth?"

Johnny stood up, straightened his shoulders, and reached for Charlie's lantern. "Come on, Chum," he said. "We've got to get these boys back home."

Chum led the way until they reached the ore-car tracks. No one spoke until they came to a section that spanned the dark chasm of a cave-in. A twelve-foot stretch of blackness lay below the narrow tracks.

"What are we gonna do now?" asked Charlie, frightened at the prospect of crossing the void. "How're we gonna get across?"

"The tracks aren't wide . . . three feet all the way across. We can straddle them," said Johnny.

"Sure, we can straddle our way across, can't we, Charlie?" asked Luke.

"Ain't there some other way?" asked Charlie, looking down at his short legs, and comparing them to Johnny's and Luke's.

"Dammit, Charlie!" shouted Johnny, wheeling around to glare at him. "What more do you want?" His angry outburst surprised even him. He suspected it had something to do with the loss of Maud. He immediately regretted his impatience.

"It's all right, Johnny," said Luke quietly. "I can get him across."

Johnny turned away; he whistled for Chum, lifted him up, and carried him across. On the other side, he waited for the boys.

Charlie set a foot on each rail and inched his way toward Johnny, on the other side of the abyss. He looked down into the blackness and nearly fell forward. He struggled to regain his balance, flailing his arms and pitching forward and backward on the rails.

"Don't look down," called Johnny. "Look straight ahead at me. Don't look down!" Luke quickly came up behind Charlie and steadied him from behind.

"Okay! Okay!" gasped Charlie. "I'm all right now."

Charlie grimaced and fixed his eyes on Johnny. With Luke holding on to Charlie's thick waist to guide him, they made it across without further incident.

As they passed the big sinkhole, they were astounded to see that the lake of water had completely disappeared. It looked like a crater at the top of a volcanic mountain, almost a quarter mile across. Nobody knew how many feet deep.

All that water is coursing through the mine at this minute, Johnny thought, *carrying Maud's body to an unknown grave.* Johnny sobbed once and shivered inside his wet slicker.

Up ahead, they saw the glow of lanterns and the sound of raucous voices coming from down the tracks.

Graywolf's men stopped suddenly and watched bug-eyed as three figures advanced toward them in the eerie moonlit fog. Jean-Paul stopped, and his men halted behind him. Big John, Nathan, Billy, Herb Norris, and Jack Tatum, having roared up the hill in pursuit of the lumber truck, made their way out in front of the group. They stood abreast together and squinted toward the oncoming figures.

"Who goes there?" called Herb.

"It's us, Charlie Tatum and—," Charlie answered excitedly.

"Quiet!" hissed Johnny. "It might be Graywolf's men."

Luke stiffened, expecting to see his father's scowling face.

"Who wants to know?" shouted Johnny.

Nathan Lightfoot and Jack Tatum broke from the crowd, running up the track toward the boys. Big John and Billy followed.

"Johnny! Son, how did *you* get here? What's happened? You found the boys!" Nathan pulled Johnny into his arms, searching with his eyes and hands for signs of injury to his son. Jack Tatum and Charlie threw their arms around each other, and both began to cry.

"It was Maud, Father. It was Maud who found Luke and Charlie, and saved their lives and mine."

Big John looked beyond the boys and down the tracks. "And where *is* Maud?" asked Big John, taking a few steps back in the direction of Maud's cabin.

Johnny laid a hand on his grandfather's arm and pulled him back. "She . . . she's gone, Grandfather." Johnny swallowed hard. "She drowned in the mine."

Big John's shoulders slumped, his eyes suddenly dark. "Dead?" he asked weakly. "Maud? Dead?"

"Yes, Grandfather," Johnny said softly. "Please, take us home now."

Herb Norris turned back toward the men who waited and listened behind Jean-Paul. They murmured among themselves, passing along the word of Old Maud's demise.

"All right, you men. You heard what happened. The boys are safe and sound. The party's over. Go on back to camp now. Tell Graywolf he'll find his boy safe, asleep in his own bed."

Jean-Paul faced his men, waving both arms toward their waiting truck. The men, sobered by what they had just seen, walked slowly back to the truck and quietly climbed aboard. Jean-Paul, his face like a mask, climbed up behind the wheel. But before he could slam the door shut, Graywolf and Sheriff Cabot stepped out of the shadows between parked trucks with rifles drawn. Graywolf reached up and pulled Jean-Paul from the cab. Jean-Paul tried to kick him, but lost his footing and fell to the ground. Graywolf pulled him up by the collar, drew back his huge fist, and drove it into Jean-Paul's face. Sheriff Cabot bent down and snapped handcuffs on Jean-Paul's wrists, then loaded his unconscious body into the bed of Graywolf's pickup and drove away without a word.

Graywolf walked over to Big John. "I been wrong about a lot of things, Big John," he said with humility. "I'm ashamed, and I apologize for the kind of man I've been in the past. I'm grateful to Johnny for findin' my boy, and I'm glad you and my neighbors were here to keep these cowards from hurtin' Old Maud," he said sincerely, gesturing toward the truck full of hangdog lumbermen.

"Maud is dead," Big John said quietly. "She died saving your son Luke, Charlie Tatum, and my Johnny. Your apologies belong to Luke, and your gratitude to Maud."

Luke stood shivering with the cold and fear of retribution. Graywolf groaned in despair. He knelt in front of his son, his eyes filled with tears. "I'm truly sorry about Old Maud, Luke. I was wrong about her *and* you. I hope you can forgive me. Could I begin from this moment to prove how much I love you, to show you I can be a good father to you and your brothers and sister, like Charlie's dad is to his family? I'd be grateful for another chance."

Luke threw his arms around his father's neck. Tom Graywolf stood up and held his son close. "I'd be much obliged if you'd take my boys home," he said to Big John. "I need to drive these hoodlums back to camp."

"Of course." Big John extended his hand to Graywolf in a gesture of forgiveness and friendship.

 *Twenty-three*

It was long after midnight when the Light-foot men returned home. Mary was waiting up. She knew right away that something was wrong, but there were four tall figures on the path from the barn and she was grateful for that. Their faces were solemn. They quietly filed past her through the open door. Mary opened her arms to her son.

"Maud is dead, Mother," said Johnny. "She found Charlie and Luke, but the water broke into the mine. Luke, Charlie, and I escaped, but Maud . . . Maud drowned."

"Oh, Johnny, Johnny," Mary cried, and pulled her son closer.

She sat at the kitchen table with Johnny while he drank a cup of hot cocoa. She could see that his heart was heavy. Nathan brought in wood for the fire and poked it back to life. Big John, his face sad and haggard, sat in his chair, watching the sparks fly up the chimney. Billy brought cups and a steaming pot of coffee from the kitchen stove, poured a cup for his father, and placed it in his languid hands.

"You need rest, Johnny," Mary said softly to her son. "Why don't you go up to bed now? We can talk about it later, when you feel better."

"No, Mother. I need to talk about it now. I need to tell you all that happened in the mine."

Nathan held a blanket to warm at the hearth while Mary helped Johnny remove his wet clothes. Nathan wrapped the blanket around Johnny, and placed his chair close to the fire. Chum slept soundly in his accustomed place beside the hearth.

Johnny related the events as they happened, from the time he left the house, including even the smallest details. He told how he'd been afraid of going into the treacherous mine in the storm, and how bad he'd felt about breaking his word to his father. Nathan and Mary exchanged understanding glances.

Johnny seemed compelled to repeat Maud's every word, describing her concerns and reactions to what was happening in the mine, as though he were etching the events of the night into his memory forever. He talked about Luke's natural abilities and of his shame for his own impatience with Charlie. The sun was rising as he spoke of his bitterness that Maud had been taken away just as they were becoming close. He felt cheated of the rich opportunity to know her better. Finally, with the image of Maud's hands slipping from the ladder, he repeated her last words, "My Bible, Johnny. Keep my Bible."

When Johnny finished his story, spent and weeping, Big John slumped back in his chair. He moaned softly while tears streamed from his eyes, streaked his face, and rolled down his neck. His voice, choked with sobs, rose voluminously in the old Micmac ancestral tradition. It reminded Johnny of the day that Maud told them the story of the tavern fire.

Finally exhausted, Johnny rose from his chair and wrapped the blanket around himself. He kissed his grandfather's wrinkled brow, went upstairs, and crawled into bed. He pulled the pillow over his head to muffle the sounds he was about to make for the first time, for the most profound loss of his young life. He howled, like his grandfather, into the pillow. He discovered for himself how much better this vocal release of sorrow made him feel. He hoped that wherever Maud was, she would hear his cry and know how he felt. He had seen her swept away in the mine, but in his heart he knew that her spirit was stronger than death. Convinced that Maud, in her infinite wisdom and power, could overcome whatever peril she faced in the mine, Johnny's eyes finally closed beneath a soothing, healing blanket of sleep, and of dreams of Maud calling his name from the echoing chambers of the mine. "My Bible, Johnny. Keep my Bible."

Twenty-four

A few days later, Nathan drove the truck up to the clearing above Mine Hill with Johnny and Big John. Herb and Billy rode in back. Herb had yet to inspect the latest devastation in the mine, and a report to the government was due.

Herb wanted to follow the Lightfoot men all the way to Maud's cabin, but Big John had other ideas.

"Sorry, Herb," Big John said when they stopped the truck. "We're obliged to go on alone. This is a family matter. Maud Fournier was my first cousin, you see. And even though her cabin is on mine property, I ask that you honor her grandfather rights, or squatter's rights, if you will, and allow us to remove her personal effects and dispose of her belongings as we see fit."

"Your cousin! Old Maud was your cousin! But how? Well, of course," sputtered Herb. "You . . . ah . . . have every right. Just be careful." Herb turned and headed to the west of the ore-car tracks to inspect the empty sinkhole.

When the Lightfoot men reached Maud's cabin, Johnny and Big John went inside, and Nathan and Billy waited outside on the steps. They didn't feel quite right about going inside Maud's home "seeing as they had never met."

The cabin was exactly as Maud had left it. Nostalgia swept over Johnny. The sweet smell of herbs and dried flowers saddened him. Crow perched on his shelf behind the cold woodstove, pecking randomly at whatever food was left in his cup, and remained silent. In the corner on a nail hung her fur robe, which she was wearing at her first meeting with Johnny. Her boots, tied together, hung close by.

On the table they found Maud's unfinished letter to Big John that began: "My dearest Cousin John. I regret . . . " Johnny was not surprised that Maud was rejecting their offer; he understood why and hoped his grandfather would, too. The small gold nugget resting on the paper made Johnny and his grandfather look at each other with puzzled expressions. "Maybe for Mr. Norris to deliver the letter," Johnny suggested.

The cabin was so full of Maud's presence that if she had come through the door of her bedchamber at that moment, Johnny wouldn't have been at all surprised.

They found the Bible on the box beside her bed. Big John carefully thumbed through its pages, his rapt expression registering happy memories from old family photographs. Halfway through he discovered Maud's simple will under the two bags of gold dust cleverly hidden in the center of the book. He read the paper, then handed it to Johnny. The will was signed "Maud Rachael Fournier," witnessed by Ezekiel Addis, Peddler. Following the directions in the will, Johnny and Big John went outside to the little courtyard. They climbed down the ladder to the now partially flooded root cellar, where they found the bag of gold nuggets and her Aunt Jane's silver mirror.

Further instructions in Maud's will directed Johnny and Big John to set fire to her little cabin just as darkness fell. "I am finished with it. As for Crow," she had written, "open the windows and doors as you set the fire to hasten his flight, but mind, he is old and may not want to leave." Outside, they watched closely, but neither saw Crow fly from the cabin.

The Lightfoot men stood clear and watched the flames lick the walls of the canyon. Within minutes the cabin roof collapsed in a great shower of sparks. In the updraft, like the soul leaving a body, flaming pieces of the little cabin blew beyond the top of the canyon, disappearing over the rim. The well in the back courtyard came into view as the cabin walls disintegrated. Johnny watched the shadows dance on the sheer walls of the canyon and remembered how, not that long ago, Maud had waited there with her lantern, hoping for his trust. So much had happened since that night when he and his injured dog had followed her into that canyon.

In the village below, the inhabitants of Beaver Creek watched the bright orange flames as they grew at the top of the mine. They whispered among themselves while they witnessed what they called the "spiritual cleansing" of the Lightfoot witch. She had redeemed her soul, they said, when she rescued the Graywolf and Tatum boys, but deep down they were glad she was gone and would walk among them no more.

Arrangements had been made with Father McCort to conduct Maud's memorial service. But a few of his parishioners complained that Maud had not been a member of the church, and that her reputation as a religious person was questionable at best. To keep peace in the parish, Father McCort agreed not to conduct the service, but he honored the Lightfoot family's request that the service be held in the church. And he suggested that Big John eulogize his cousin.

Big John Lightfoot rose to the occasion. He told Maud's tragic story, and of his family's relationship to her parents, with warmth and compassion. Except for a couple of old-timers, no one presently living in Beaver Creek remembered the tavern fire or Maud's parents. But Big John asked those present—sympathetic but mostly curious villagers—to put aside their past superstitious beliefs about Maud Fournier. He asked that she be remembered as a victim of tragic circumstances who had wanted nothing more than to be accepted by her people, and who had made the ultimate sacrifice on their behalf.

Maud's considerable life savings—in the form of gold— were appraised by Big John's bank in Halifax. An officious young banker met with Big John to certify Maud's gift to Johnny's college education. Later, meeting with Beaver Creek officials, the banker informed them of the windfall from Maud Fournier's estate: a new school to be built for the children of Beaver Creek, with a swimming pool to replace the old sinkhole in the mine. There was only one addition that Big John insisted upon: A bronze plaque, commemorating Maud's gift, was to be mounted on a square granite slab and surrounded by a small garden on the new school's front lawn for everyone to see.

When the project was completed, the Lightfoot family gathered, with many more villagers than had attended the memorial service, to install the plaque. It read: *In loving memory of Maud Rachael Fournier, born 1875, died 1943. A generous, loving, and beautiful woman, Maud will remain in the hearts and minds of her people forever.*

Epilogue

Since the night Maud was lost, no one ever again ventured into the "haunted" mine. Herb Norris retired from his position as gatekeeper. The gate was never repaired. Its twisted pieces lie on either side of lower Mine Hill, and poison ivy has wound its tendrils through the rusted remains. The gatehouse stands empty and forlorn. Ragged remnants of white curtains flutter eerily through one of its broken windows, and the front door swings on creaking hinges with every breeze. An aura of death and decay hangs over the place and drapes it in vaporous silence. Brush grows among the rocks and outcroppings, but, strangely, no large animals come to drink from the mine's little ponds.

During Johnny's second year at university, his grandfather took sick with pneumonia and died just hours before Johnny could reach home. Big John was buried beside his wife, Ruth, in the little Lightfoot family plot on the hill overlooking Loon Lake. Chum had earlier succumbed to an infection from a penetration of porcupine quills. He, too, was buried in the family plot.

After his grandfather's funeral service, Johnny waited for the bus at Milligan's Store to take him back to the Junction station. A new crop of rowdy schoolchildren streamed into the store to buy after-school treats. The old men around the potbellied stove were annoyed at having their game of checkers disrupted, and one raised his cane threateningly at the children.

"Go on home now 'fore it gets dark. Old Maud'll be waitin' for you on the road yonder," he cackled.

"You can't scare me, old man," one of the bigger boys piped up. "Old Maud's dead—drowned in the mine years back." The other children giggled nervously.

"That's what you think, you little whelp. Her *body* was never found," he said with a wink. "Fire and water weren't no match for Old Maud's magic, ha ha."

Johnny watched from his departing bus as the children quietly left Milligan's Store, their treats forgotten. Huddled together in the cold blue twilight, they walked quickly down the snowy, winding road toward home, glancing over their shoulders as they went.

Acknowledgments

I wish to thank my friends and colleagues at the Camden Writers Round Table who encouraged me with their enthusiastic support and professional critiques: Cynthia Renfrette-Barlow, Mark Battista, Gig Kerr, Cathy McClain, Elizabeth Olsen, Gail Portnoy, Judy Driscoll Winchenbaugh, Bess Urbahn, and all the other member-writers whose names are too many to mention here.

A special thanks to my editor and friend, Barbara A. Feller Roth, for her professionalism, hard work, her strong sense of pacing, her undaunting faith in the story, and for caring so deeply; and to Marti Reed, Erika Pfander, Amber Rattina, and Caitlin Throne for taking the time for readings.

My gratitude to Sherie Schmauder for her early interest, help, and encouragement.

I appreciate my children's sense of pride in their mother's accomplishment; I can't adequately thank my husband, Tom Laurent, who loved the story from its inception, and who was always confident that I could write it.